5/17/12

the chic shall inherit the earth

an all about us novel

SHELLEY ADINA

FaithWords

NEW YORK
BOSTON
NASHVILLE

Scripture quotations marked NIV are taken from the HOLY BIBLE, NEW INTERNATIONAL VERSION®. Copyright © 1973, 1978, 1984 International Bible Society. Used by permission of Zondervan. All rights reserved.

The "NIV" and "New International Version" trademarks are registered in the United States Patent and Trademark Office by International Bible Society. Use of either trademark requires the permission of International Bible Society.

FaithWords
Hachette Book Group
237 Park Avenue
New York, NY 10017

www.faithwords.com.

The FaithWords name and logo are trademarks of Hachette Book Group.

Printed in the United States of America

First Edition: January 2010
10 9 8 7 6 5 4 3 2 1

Library of Congress Cataloging-in-Publication Data

Adina, Shelley.
  The chic shall inherit the earth / by Shelley Adina. — 1st ed.
    p. cm.
  Summary: At San Francisco's exclusive Spencer Academy, seventeen-year-old Lissa gains popularity when she replaces her nemesis, Vanessa, on the senior Cotillion committee, but graduation and major decisions about the future loom.
  ISBN 978-0-446-17964-5
  [1. Interpersonal relations—Fiction. 2. Christian life—Fiction. 3. Balls (Parties)—Fiction. 4. Pregnancy—Fiction. 5. College choice—Fiction. 6. High schools—Fiction. 7. Schools—Fiction. 8. San Francisco (Calif.)—Fiction.] I. Title.
  PZ7.A261147Ch 2010
  [Fic]—dc22   2009015625

For my readers, with love and thanks

acknowledgments

Over the course of this series, I've had the opportunity to work with some of the most professional people in the business. My agent, Jennifer Jackson, who is the voice of reason no matter how chaotic things get. My editor, Anne Goldsmith Horch, whose cheery notes and incisive editing are a constant encouragement. The art department at FaithWords—have I said lately how fabulous the All About Us covers are? I have? Then let me say it again—you guys rock! Preston Cannon and Echo Music, who run the series site at allaboutusbooks.net; Shanon Stowe, who keeps on top of publicity; Miriam Parker, who whips blog tours out of a hat and is a friendly presence on Facebook; Katie Schaber, who always has the answer, no matter how weird the question . . . It has been an honor and a really good time working with you all. Thank you.

the chic
shall inherit
the earth

Perfume and incense bring joy to the heart,
and the pleasantness of one's friend springs
from his earnest counsel.
—*Proverbs 27:9 (NIV)*

chapter 1

ET ME PUT IT right out there: I'm no sports fan—
unless you count surfing, which is more of an attitude
to life than a sport. I used to think that there were
some things you just knew. But if God were a major league
pitcher, He'd be the kind of guy who threw curveballs just to
keep you on your toes. To catch you off guard. To prove you
wrong about everything you thought.

Which is essentially what happened to us all during the
last term of our senior year at Spencer Academy.

My name is Lissa Evelyn Mansfield—yes, I'm back again.
Did you miss me? Because, seriously, this last term of high
school before my friends and I graduated was so crazed, so
unpredictable, that I had to write it all down to try and make
sense of it.

But, hey, let's take a moment here. The words *last term of
senior year* need some respect, not to mention celebration.
They need to be paused over and savored. Excuse me.

Okay, I'm back.

The term began in April, and by the time our first set of midterms (or thirdterms, as my roommate Gillian Chang calls them, since we get three sets of exams every term) rolled around at the beginning of May, it was just beginning to sink in that there were only seven weeks of high school left. Seven weeks until freedom. Adulthood. Summer vacation. Adulthood. Home.

Adulthood.

Eek.

"Sarah Lawrence is stalking me," Gillian moaned from where she sat on her bed in our dorm room. "Here's another letter." She fished an envelope out of the pile of mail in her lap and waved it.

I looked up from my MacBook Air, where I was checking e-mail. "Don't let Emily Overton hear you. She got turned down and her roommate has had to keep her away from open windows for the last month."

"But I already told them no twice. What's it going to take?"

"You could fail some exams." I'm always willing to offer a helpful suggestion. "They can't help it if they covet your fearsome brain."

"So does Harvard. And Princeton. Not to mention Stanford and Columbia and Juilliard." She threw her hands in the air so that the letter flew over her shoulder and bounced off the headboard. "How am I supposed to pick just one? Can I spend a year at each school? I could be a career transfer student."

"I'm glad I don't have your decisions to make," I told her with absolute honesty. "If all those schools were after me, I'd run away and hide."

"I've got to figure out what I'm doing with my life." She

glanced at me. "Or maybe I should say, what God wants me to do with my life."

"There's the kicker." I nodded sagely. "I understand about waiting on the Lord, but . . . He knows about registration deadlines, doesn't He?"

"Oh, yeah. He knows. I keep asking Him, and He keeps thinking about it. Maybe He wants me to figure out what I want, first. But that's the impossible part."

Poor Gillian. She has the kind of brain schools fight over for their research programs. But she's also a music prodigy—hence the acceptance from Juilliard. Then, to complicate things even more, she also has quite the talent for drawing, and ever since she met my friend Kaz Griffin, her dream has been to create a graphic novel starring a kick-butt Asian girl with a secret identity. Kaz, in case you haven't met him, is my best friend from my old high school in Santa Barbara. He's been trying to get his graphic novel published for, like, *years*, with no success. But I have to hand it to him. He never gives up.

Anyway. Gillian.

"You could always do pre-med at Harvard and minor in art or music," I suggested. "You know you're going to need a release valve from all that scientific pressure. It would be good to have the right-brain kind of classes to turn to."

Gillian pushed the stack of mail off her lap and leaned back against the mound of colorful silk pillows. The letter from Sarah Lawrence crumpled somewhere underneath. "But then how will I know if I'm any good?"

"Um, your grades? Not to mention, if you got an acceptance from Juilliard, you're good. Full stop, as Mac would say."

Lady Lindsay MacPhail, aka Mac, was a student here at

Spencer for two terms, and she's one of our little group of friends. She's gone back to live in London until the end of term, when she'll return to her family's castle in Scotland, and she has none of these questions about her life. She knows exactly what degree she's going to get, when she'll get it, and what she'll be doing after that: making the Strathcairn Hotel and Corporate Retreat Center the go-to place for world-class events in the UK.

I envy people who have their future in a laser sight. I'm still trying to figure out what to wear tomorrow.

"What do teachers know?" Gillian asked. I don't think she was looking for the answer to that one. "If I'm going to find out whether I'm really any good, I have to try to get into an art program and give it everything I've got. Try to get an exhibition. Or a publisher. Live in a garret and try to make it as an artist."

"That sounds scary."

"I know." She sighed. "Medical school is the easy path, grasshopper."

Only Gillian Chang would say something like that.

I turned back to my notebook and saw that while we'd been talking, a message from Kaz had popped up in my inbox.

....

✉

To: lmansfield@spenceracad.edu
From: kazg@hotmail.com
Date: May 4, 2010
Re: Ow

I am so regretting pushing off physics until senior year. My brain hurts. What was I thinking? Instead of grabbing my board and heading for the beach, I'm stuck down here in my room writing equations I don't know the answers to.

Does the Jumping Loon tutor over the phone? Can you ask her? I'll give her anything she wants, including full use of my studly body, if she'll just say the magic words that will unveil the meaning of x and y, not to mention z.

Life, I've got a handle on. X is a mystery.

Kaz

....

I looked over my shoulder. "Kaz wants to know if you do physics tutoring over the phone. He says you can do what you want with his body if you help him." I paused when she didn't look up from a Neiman Marcus catalog. "I didn't know you were interested in his body. Does Jeremy know about this?"

"That sounds like a jealous remark." She flipped a page. "Ooh, nice dress. Chloé does summer so well. Which reminds me, if we're going on a Senior Cotillion dress safari, we'd better start soon."

I was not to be sidetracked, no matter how tempting the bait. "Is something going on with you and Kaz?"

She put the catalog down and rolled her eyes to the ceiling. "Yes. Yes, there is."

I sat there as stunned as if someone had upended a bucket of seawater over me.

Kaz and Gillian? What? How is that possible? When did—

What is the matter with you? Kaz is your friend. You aren't . . . like that. If he's interested in Gillian, it's none of your business.

Poor Jeremy.

"Lissa. Lissa, come back to me." I blinked at her. My face felt frozen. "For crying out loud, get a grip." She was trying not to laugh and not succeeding very well. "He's teasing you. He's helping me with a plaster mold of his hand for my art project, okay? That's all."

"A mold. Of his hand. And you don't have guys' hands any closer than Santa Barbara?"

"He has interesting hands, which you'd know if you ever paid any attention."

Of course he did. And of course I did. Pay attention to him, I mean. He was my best friend. We e-mailed each other, like, twenty times a week.

"And Jeremy's hands aren't interesting?"

She picked up the catalog and flipped another page. "Write him back and tell him of course I'll tutor him. We can start tonight if he's desperate."

Hm. Poor Jeremy, indeed. What was going on here? "He wants to know the meaning of *x*."

"Don't we all. Some of us wait for the universe to reveal it to us. And some of us wouldn't know it if the universe dropped it on our heads."

"What's your point?"

But my friend, who usually has all the answers, didn't reply.

chapter 2

HAVING A BOYFRIEND can be like having a root canal—once you've had one, you want everyone else to go through the same experience so they know what you're talking about.

I'm not down on boyfriends, honest. I've had a few. And if I had half a clue about how to get a nice guy's attention and keep it, I'd be the first one to jump on the bandwagon with Gillian and with Carly, who is joined at the lip with Brett Loyola, the captain of the rowing team. They've been together almost exactly a year now, to the continuing astonishment of Vanessa Talbot and her glossy posse.

Personally, I think most of Vanessa's catty gossip about Carly is a case of sour grapes. Brett's period of mourning after V. dumped him last year lasted, like, a nanosecond before Carly got his attention. That's gotta sting.

Carly's roommate, Shani Hanna, is in a long-distance relationship with Danyel Johnstone, one of my friends from Santa Barbara. She doesn't date guys from school, mostly because she's taken, but even if she wasn't, she turned down a prince during fall term and now all the guys here are scared to ask her out. I heard two seniors talking behind the stacks in the library only last week: "He had a nine-figure net worth and a private security detail and she broke up with him. What are my chances?"

I didn't step out from behind the English Novelists of the Nineteenth Century to tell them, "Zero, babe." Danyel is adorable—think Corbin Bleu with a surfboard—and she'd rather get one e-mail from him than spend a whole evening clubbing with anybody else. Danyel is Kaz's best friend, which is why Shani doesn't mind sharing stuff like that with me. I've known Danyel my whole life, and if she could do a mind-meld with me and suck everything I know about him out of my cortex, she would.

I'm really lucky when it comes to friends. With a bud like Kaz, and with my girlfriends' boyfriends around all the time, I'm not hurting for male company. It's just that some-times when Carly looks at Brett and they drift off into this personal universe that doesn't have anyone in it but them-selves . . . it's hard not to want it, too. Hard not to go bug the Lord to send me someone like that. Yes, I do know He has more important things to manage. But still.

Truth? The simple fact is that after what happened with Callum McCloud last year, I'm not sure I'm girlfriend mate-rial. He called me needy and clingy, yet we'd hardly had one date and he was trying to get my clothes off. I'm not needy. I am responsible and popular . . . okay, *was* popular, if you're a stickler about tenses . . . and I have a great family and friends to love. Needy. Pffft. I'm disproving that one as we speak, since there is no one in my life at present to need.

Case closed, Callum McCloud, you jerk.

I gave up on e-mail and snapped my notebook shut. Gillian had separated her mail into neat piles: do, read, and toss. The letter from Sarah Lawrence went into the recycle bin next to the door, along with the rest of the "toss" stack. One down, half a dozen eager colleges to go. Lucky thing we were getting lots of practice in deadlines and decisions. For Gillian, the first were getting close, and the second had to be made soon.

Me, I was already set: UC Santa Barbara, with a major in literature. (And a minor in surfing, as Gillian would point out.) After hitting the short list for the Hearst Medal in writing, the scouts for all the California universities had come knocking at my door. It felt good, but my mind was already made up. There was only one place where I wanted to kick off this business of being an adult: the place where I'd grown up.

Now that my parents were dating again (long story) and my dad's big adventure epic, *The Middle Window*, was in global release and on its way to theaters in Japan and Australia, he'd moved from Marin back to Santa Barbara to wait for Hollywood to send him a script he couldn't turn down. So that was where I'd be heading right after graduation.

Home.

Gillian glanced at the clock. "Almost seven. You ready?"

"Just gotta brush my hair."

Five minutes later we were on our way to prayer circle, which has happened every Tuesday night since Gillian's and my first term here. Not that I deserve any credit. She's the one who organizes it, and the rest of us follow along, being thankful that she does.

I could hear Shani's and Carly's voices on the marble staircase above us, and a few seconds later they clattered into view.

"Nice sandals, girlfriend," I said to Shani with an admiring glance at her perfectly pedicured feet. "Don't tell me. Prada?"

"Not even close. Those days are gone." Remember the prince? When Shani refused to go through with an arranged marriage to him, her parents disowned her. They cleaned out her room and sent all her stuff to charity, leaving only what she had in her closet here at Spencer. She hasn't really heard from them since. Harsh or what? Needless to say, we've become the closest thing to sisters to her, trying to make up a family for her right here.

"No," she went on, "these are Miu Miu, and I snapped them up on eBay for next to nothing."

Carly nodded with approval. "I like the gold. It goes great with your skin tone."

"Black and gold, my favorite combination." Shani gave us all a smug smile at her superior bargain-hunting skills. You'd never know she owned a dress Karl Lagerfeld had designed for her personally. Like she said, those days were gone forever.

In Room 216, we dragged the chairs into a circle and people slowly trickled in. Gillian sat at the spinet in the corner and proceeded to turn a worship tune into a work of art. When Jeremy came in, she didn't even look at the keyboard as she smiled at him, and her fingers just kept finding all those handfuls of rapid notes. Brett came in shortly afterward, trailed by a couple of the guys from the rowing team. Don't get excited—I think they follow him into the bathroom, too, not to mention lunch and half his classes. They'd probably carry his backpack if he let them. With the school's sportsman's trophy 99 percent locked up and the unofficial title of Hottest Guy in Pacific Heights, I suppose it's inevitable that

Brett would have a posse. As it is, he's as nice to them as he is to everyone—and ditches them whenever he can, so he can hang out with Carly. The guy does have his limits.

Two juniors and one very brave freshman filled up the circle, and Gillian wound up with a flourish. "Thanks for coming, everyone. Who wants to start?"

"I will," I said. She slid into her seat between me and Jeremy, and I closed my eyes. "Father, thanks for these prayer circles. Some days, knowing that I get to sit down with You and my friends here is what keeps me going. Thanks for Gillian, and for putting the idea of a prayer circle in her heart in the first place." I took a breath. "Father, Gillian's the one I want to pray for tonight. She's got a lot of decisions to make, and she wants to do the right thing and wait on You to tell her what You want for her. Please let her hear Your voice clearly. In Jesus' name."

People murmured "amen" and Gillian leaned over and bumped my shoulder gently with hers. *Thank you.* With a smile, my eyes closed, I bumped her back. *Don't mention it.*

A laptop snapped open, and a second later I heard Danyel Johnstone's familiar voice. He sent Shani a podcast or a video every week so he could join us by proxy. As he prayed for all of us he knew by name, part of my mind wondered why Kaz never did that. I'd have loved to hear him pray with us. His voice had deepened as he got more mature, and I never got tired of hearing it. And what better way to use your voice than in prayer circle? I'd send him an e-mail as soon as I got back to our room, I decided. Maybe it had just never occurred to him.

After we'd gone all around the circle, skipping over the crew guys, who never said a word when they came, Gillian played while we belted out her current favorite praise song.

"I love listening to you sing that," I told Shani as we collected our handbags. "I can't believe they didn't snap you up when you auditioned for the chorus."

"I'm not a chorus type," she admitted. "I'm a soloist, and that wasn't what they were looking for. I'm okay with it. I'd rather sing with my friends, anyway, than have a whole bunch of people staring at me."

"I hear ya. Especially since you gotta believe they'd be thinking of . . . you know."

The prince. He was like Brett's hangers-on, only invisible. Everywhere Shani went, the story of the girl who had turned down the Lion Throne of Yasir went, too. You could ignore it, but you just couldn't shake it.

"Who's coming to Starbucks?" Carly asked.

It was a couple of blocks' walk down one of San Francisco's steeper hills, which is why I could knock back an entire grande-with-whip mocha and suffer no ill effects from the calories. The climb back up the hill to the school wiped them out as if they had never been.

As we crowded out the double front doors and onto the stone steps that led down to the school's gravel drive, Vanessa Talbot passed us on the way in. The limo she'd just climbed out of bowled away toward the gates, and she tugged her Furla shoulder bag higher and swung an Elie Tahari shopping bag onto the other arm.

"Vanessa's been out shopping alone?" I murmured to Carly. "Is that even possible? How can she function with no one to fetch her coffee and hold her bag while she tries things on?"

Carly coughed to cover up a giggle. Sorry about the catty remarks. But Vanessa Talbot is a sore point with me, after what she did to me last year.

"Finished praying for the night?" she asked sweetly as she passed us.

"Yes." Gillian's reply was sarcasm-free. Sometimes that is the only way to deal with nastiness. "Unless you want us to put in a good word for you."

Vanessa rolled her eyes. "Like I'd ever need anything from you losers. How does it feel to be on the outside again, looking in?"

Out of the corner of my eye, I saw something as the door swung shut on the last word.

"What?" Carly said. "It's too late for that snappy comeback I see on the tip of your tongue."

"Did you see that?" I wagged a thumb over my shoulder as we walked down the drive toward the wrought-iron gates, where, sure enough, a photographer lounged in a beat-up subcompact, his telephoto lens propped on the open window frame. One or more were always there, trying to catch a thousand-dollar shot of one of the celebrity offspring or children of minor royalty like Vanessa. "Vanessa was wearing Apple Bottoms jeans."

Carly swung around to look at the front door, but of course the other girl was long gone. "Impossible. You must have been hallucinating."

"The mushrooms in the soup at supper were morels, not anything stronger," I retorted. "I know my jeans, and that girl was not wearing her usual custom Stella McCartneys."

"She has been packing on the pounds," Brett said as we headed down the hill. "But she always was too skinny."

Shani gave him a look. "Everyone knows that the camera puts twenty-five pounds on you. She's photographed all the time. Of course she's going to be skinny. If she were bigger than a size zero, she'd look like a Dumpster on SeenOn-dot-com."

"Whatever." Brett obviously thought of body mass in terms of how much torque a person could put on an oar, not how they looked in front of a camera. "She just looks healthier with a few extra on her, that's all."

Healthy wasn't the word for it. She hadn't just been wearing Apple Bottoms. That babydoll top wasn't the norm for her, either. It was neither sleek nor chic. Hm. "Guess that's the reason for the emergency shopping trip," I mused out loud as we passed the eclectic little shops on Fillmore Street. "Maybe someone commented on her recent wardrobe choices, and she had to take corrective action."

"What, like you?" Gillian said. "Stop obsessing, already."

I clamped my mouth shut on what would only sound defensive. I did not obsess about Vanessa. Why would I? She had her posse—or what was left of them. Dani Lavigne was doing an exchange term in Paris (and spending way more time clubbing with her famous cousin on her European tour than studying, if the tabs were to be believed). Emily Overton hovered on the fringes of our group. None of us were sure if she really wanted to be friends with us, or if, as Shani suspected, she was a deep-cover spy for the enemy. DeLayne Geary, who had been one of Vanessa's second-tier friends, was about the only one left who had the right to walk down the corridors with her, or to sit at the prize table in the window in the dining room.

I had no desire to sit there anymore. My friends were the real kind—like gold tried by fire. We've been through a lot together since junior year. A symbol like that table in the dining room was not only unnecessary, it was sort of silly.

At Starbucks, I ordered the aforementioned grande-with-whip mocha and when we all had our drinks, we settled into the corner group of chairs around a low table. "So, Jeremy, when are you going up to UC Davis for orientation?" Carly asked him.

"I can't believe you've made up your mind," Gillian moaned into her cup. "How can it be that easy?"

"I've always known what I wanted to be," Jeremy said simply. "And the best veterinary program is at Davis. All I had to do was get in."

"Augh." Gillian gulped her caramel macchiato. "I have a spreadsheet of pros and cons. A cost/benefit analysis. Even a photo slideshow from every school's "Student Life" page. And still I can't make up my mind."

"It's not about student life, though, is it?" Carly asked. "It's about your life, and what God wants you to do with it."

"That's the point I always arrive at," Gillian admitted. "I want to wait on God, but I can't wait too long or I miss the registration deadline. I mean, He gave me this brain for a reason. I just have to figure out the best place to use it."

"That's gotta be hard," Shani said. "I mean, granted, I'm new at being a Christian. But it never occurred to me to ask God what He wants me to do. I just went ahead and applied to Harvard Business School, got in, got my scholarship, and I'm good to go."

"You make that sound as easy as Jeremy did," I said. "But I know you've been working like a demented person for months and months to get in. And don't even talk to me about your application essay. That was grueling for all of us."

"And I appreciate every bit of help you guys gave me." She flashed a rare Shani smile, the kind that lit her up and softened the cut planes of her face—the ones that had photographed so well in our *People* spread last fall—into real beauty. "But, Gillian, you're, like, solid. Don't you think you're going to make the right decision just because you belong to God?"

"Not necessarily." Gillian's gaze fell to Jeremy's foot, crossed over his knee, his sneaker beginning to bounce up and down as the caffeine kicked in. "I wouldn't want to make a big decision like this without knowing it was in His will for me. It's fine to make up my mind on the little things, like what classes to take and stuff. But a big thing like college? Nuh-uh."

"Even the classes are messing you up," I pointed out. "Like taking art last year when you never did it seriously before. It showed you there was a fork in the road. That's where all this angst started."

Gillian nodded and dimpled at me. "That Kaz. It's all his fault. If it weren't for him telling me I had talent, I'd have let that graphic arts class stay dropped when I dumped it for a personal trainer."

"I'm glad you didn't," Brett put in. "I wouldn't trade the portrait you did of Carly for anything."

"At least some good came out of Nazareth, then," she quipped. "You can tell my parents all about that when they fly out here to lecture me personally."

Knowing Gillian's parents, I had a feeling she wasn't kidding.

chapter 3

CARLY CAUGHT UP with me after Phys.Ed.— volleyball for me, soccer for her. I hadn't seen much of her since Tuesday, mostly because Gillian had to turn in a ten-page English midterm. If Gillian could have chained me by the ankle to my bed for twenty-four-hour coaching, she'd have done it. As it was, the poor girl was so stressed that I'd have done practically anything to make her feel better. Helping her with what she called "the dead white guys with verbal diarrhea" was the least I could do.

Though I didn't think Keats and Shelley had verbal diarrhea. I thought their poetry was beautiful.

"I got a note from Mac this morning." Carly swung her backpack onto her left shoulder as we crossed the playing field, heading for the dorm.

"Yeah? I haven't heard from her since last week. Cool that they got their grant from the whatever-it-was, huh?"

"Society for Self-Sustaining Estates."

"Say that five times fast."

"So now her parents will be up to their eyes in torn-out plumbing and giant gas piping for the commercial kitchen. But that wasn't what she wrote to me about this morning."

"What? Oh, wait." I held up a hand. "Alasdair Gibson's coming for the weekend."

"No such luck. I guess he's studying pretty hard, and getting from Edinburgh to London isn't so easy when you're as poor as he is. She can't wait to be finished with school. I'm sure she's packed already."

"Of course she is. They sold the London townhouse, remember? So if it wasn't Alasdair, what else is up?"

Carly didn't answer for a second. "I wrote to ask her about something. She was answering it."

I eyed her as we walked over the grass, still green and thick from the sprinklers and the San Francisco fog that kept it from burning up in the late spring and summer. "And that something would be . . . ?"

"You know how Gillian is all tweaked out about picking a college?"

"Do I. I swear, her needle is buried in the red zone. I'm trying to feed her vitamin B complex to bring the stress levels down."

"Want to give me some?"

I stopped walking and gazed at her in astonishment. "Not you, too. I thought you had it all figured out."

"There was a welcome letter from Parsons in my mail this morning."

"Parsons School of Design? That's New York, right? Wow. Congratulations."

"But I already got the one from FIDM."

Pause. "Oh." Now I got it. The campus of the Fashion Institute of Design and Merchandising that Carly wanted to go to was in L.A. Brett planned to go to Stanford because Carly's dad had his heart set on her going to Berkeley, like he did. In Brett's mind, even on opposite sides of the Bay, they'd still be close enough to see each other.

New York, on the other hand, was not close. Neither was L.A.

"What does your gut tell you?" I asked her as we resumed trekking across the grass.

"My gut and Mac both tell me I shouldn't factor Brett into my decision. But my heart tells me something different."

"And the heart is the strongest part of the girl we know and love. Oops. Sorry. Didn't mean to make you blush."

"That's why I wanted to talk to Gillian. Maybe we can pray for each other and get the Lord's attention that way. Because, honestly, I don't know how to make up my mind and make everyone happy."

"You have to live with you. That's the person you should make happy."

"And then there's my dad," she went on as if I hadn't spoken. "You know how he is."

I did. "Have you given him the news flash about FIDM?"

She shook her head. "Why invite trouble when I haven't decided yet? Maybe I should tell him about Parsons. Then if I decide to go to L.A., it'll look great in comparison."

"Man," I said on a sigh. "Can adulthood be any more complicated than this?"

"Meanwhile, there's my mom." Now it was Carly's turn to give a big sigh, blowing it up through her wispy bangs.

"Oh, help. Now what?"

"She and Richard Vigil have picked a new date for their wedding."

"When, this summer?"

"Not even. The Saturday of Memorial Day weekend. She says it's so I can fly out and back without missing any school. Hint, hint."

"She'd be right . . . if you plan to go."

"Uh-huh."

I waited for a second. "And? Do you?"

I thought about Christmas, when she'd flown to Scotland with us rather than be her mother's bridesmaid at a Christmas Eve wedding. Mr. Aragon, her dad, tried to hide the fact that he was still in love with his ex-wife, even though she was trying to marry another guy, and Carly, loyal girl that she is, wouldn't hurt her dad for anything. Yeah, he's old-fashioned and sometimes heavy-handed and strict, but he loves her to pieces.

"If I stand up in that church with her, I'll be betraying my dad and everything he feels for her."

Carly's not the betraying kind. Hence the problem.

"But, leaving him out of the equation, how do you feel about her?"

She glanced at me as we waited for the light. The playing field, the field house, and all the Phys.Ed. and dance classes are a block away from the main building. In the winter we take the rain tunnel back and forth, but on a beautiful day like today it felt great to be outside, with the San Francisco Bay sparkling in the sun in the distance.

"That would be like taking Brett out of the school equation, Lissa. It can't be done."

"Maybe you should try. If it weren't for your dad's feelings, would you do it?"

After a long pause, she said slowly, "Probably. I mean, at least Richard Vigil stuck around after the Christmas debacle. And this house they bought—it has studio space, like he really means to support her art."

"Well, then? If the guy honestly cares about her, so what if he looks like Duran Duran on their reunion tour?"

She made a face. "They'd make me be in the pictures. Imagine being in the same frame."

"That is the downside. But the upside is, you could have a relationship with her again. Maybe. If you wanted."

"That's the upside?" She began to walk faster. "You're talking about the woman who left me and Antony behind to go teach art on cruise ships and find herself. She didn't do much thinking about a relationship then."

"Still." Just how far could I butt into her business? At the same time, she'd brought it up. If she didn't want me to give her my opinion, she wouldn't have done that, right? "Think about it. The wedding, I mean. That's only, like, three weeks away. Sometimes there's a big difference between doing something out of love and doing something because it's the right thing to do."

At the bottom of the stairs up to the girls' dorm, she stopped. A muscle twitched in the smooth line of her jaw as she chewed the inside of her lip. I'm not sure I wanted to know what she wasn't letting herself say. Her mom is Carly's most vulnerable point, and talking about her is fraught with traps that you can't avoid.

"I know. 'Bye, Lissa."

"See you at lunch? Got any plans this afternoon before you catch the train?"

But she ran up the stairs and didn't answer me.

GILLIAN WASN'T IN our room, and when she didn't answer my text, I figured she was busy with something more important than what to do with our Friday afternoon.

I was thinking about the dress safari, myself. Spencer

Academy doesn't have a traditional prom or graduation
dance. Instead, it has the Senior Cotillion, all the details
of which are arranged by a committee of juniors under the
management of one senior. And all of us had known who
that would be from the moment school started in the fall.

You guessed it. Vanessa Talbot.

The mover and shaker. The social director of everything
that was anything at the school. The ultimate control freak.

Not that I wanted to be the one commanding the troops
of wide-eyed juniors with a languid wave of my manicured
fingers. Uh-uh. But it would have been nice to at least get
the chance to put my name in the hat.

As it was, Vanessa wore the hat. Period.

Still, it meant my Friday afternoons and weekends were
free for fun things like hanging out with my friends and
shopping for a dress. I could even go home to Santa Barbara
or plan a jaunt to Rodeo Drive with my mom if I felt like it.
People who needed to be in the spotlight had deeper issues
going on. I didn't have issues. I had a life.

Feeling better after this pep talk, I changed out of my
plaid skirt and white button-down blouse and into a pair
of comfortable jeans and a ruffled Free People tank. And
since Fridays deserved to be celebrated, I put on a Badgley
Mischka crystal necklace that filled the scoop neckline with
sparkle.

I ran down the stairs toward the dining room, slowing in
the corridor when Emily Overton came out of the adminis-
trative office and fell into step beside me.

"Hi, Lissa. TGIF, huh? I like your necklace."

"Thanks. I was in Hot Rocks one day last spring and fell
in love with it. Have you ever been there? It's like Ali Baba's
cave. Or like Portobello Road, only for jewelry."

"No. I hate shopping."

Um, okay.

"Mostly because it depresses me. When you're forty pounds overweight, nothing fits and you just go away feeling disgusted."

When we were kids, my sister Jolie refused to hang out at the community pool for the same reason. If she went swimming, it was on our beach, where she'd rather freeze in the open ocean than expose herself in a bathing suit to the local kids. "But you have a personal trainer, don't you? And a dietician?"

She shrugged. "It's genetic. Nothing I can do about it."

Did she really believe that, or was it a handy excuse? I pushed open the dining room door and held it for her. "I bet there is." She frowned and glanced at me as if she hadn't expected to be contradicted. Which was probably true. "I've seen your binder with your diet plan. I bet there's some stuff in there that tastes good. And if it doesn't, you could experiment, like they have us do in cookery class."

"Cooking is boring," she said. "Besides, what do you care what you eat? You're a size two."

"*That's* genetic. I take no credit for it. But I try not to mess up, which is all too easy on days there are cupcakes." Emily nodded, as though the cupcakes were her weakness, too. "And it helps to find a balance to the eating, like playing volleyball and doing gymnastics and walking to places. Lucky thing I like salad."

"I don't. Anyway. That wasn't what I wanted to talk about." We took trays and considered the offerings on display. "Burger bar," Emily said happily. "I love Fridays."

So did I. I loved cheese and crispy bacon and big heaps of fried onions. But why would anyone listen to what I said if my actions didn't back it up? I closed my eyes to the temptations of the fryer and began to build a salmon burger with lots of lettuce and roasted red pepper and a tiny bit of wasabi. Emily looked from that to the cheeseburger with bacon and avocado. Then, with a sigh, she grabbed the serving tongs and began to build a salmon burger. I smothered a smile and asked the guy behind the counter to make both of us fruit smoothies.

We found a table in the sun—not in the window, because that was forbidden, but close. Had I gotten out of class that much earlier than everyone else? Where was everyone? Around us, tables began to fill up as students trickled in, some still in uniform, and some in civvies like me.

"So, what did you want to talk about?" I took a big bite of salmon burger. Like everything else Dining Services produced (with the notable exception of the morning oatmeal, which I couldn't bring myself to eat), it was delicious.

Emily nibbled at the foccacia bread on top of her salmon. "I just wondered . . . what you would do if . . . you were in a certain situation."

"What kind of situation?" Ahhh, good wasabi. Breathe in through the nose, out through the mouth.

"If you knew . . . thought you knew something about somebody." She breathed in, then out, too. "Something really bad. That might get them expelled. Would you tell?"

"Tell who?"

"Anybody. Ms. Curzon, maybe." The headmistress.

"Depends on whether it involved fire, blood, or illegal substances."

"I'm trying to be serious here, Lissa."

"So am I. Those are the only circumstances where the school expels automatically." And how did I know this, you ask? From personal experience. Not that I'd ever been expelled. But I sure tried hard at one point, during my first term here.

"No, it doesn't involve anything like that," she said slowly. "Except maybe the blood part. I wouldn't know."

I cut her a sideways glance. "Somebody's not out there hurting anyone, are they?"

"No, no. Nothing like that. It's more of a . . . a moral thing. That's why I asked you. Because you know about stuff like that."

"What, moral things?"

"Yeah."

That was a switch. Usually Gillian got to field the philosophy and ethics questions from people. "You're not giving me much to go on. Can you be more specific?"

The doors swung open and Vanessa and DeLayne swept in. Since Emily and I were facing them, we saw their gazes rake over us and Vanessa's face pinch up as though she'd stepped in a canine landmine on the grass.

"Honestly, Emily, how desperate *are* you?" she murmured as she passed us.

Emily turned as white as a table napkin. She shoved her chair back and left the dining room at a fast walk, practically mowing down Gillian and Jeremy in the doorway.

Gillian caught my gaze and came over, slinging her cardie over the back of the chair across from me. "What was that all about?"

"I have absolutely no idea." I pushed Emily's abandoned tray all the way to the end of the table. "She was talking in riddles, and then Vanessa scared her off. I'm glad you guys are here."

At least with Gillian, a person knew where she stood.

chapter 4

A DRESS for the Senior Cotillion is probably the most important of one's high school career. It will be seen by everyone, including the media, and you can make or break your rep on WhoWhatWear.com with one mistaken choice. This is why you need people like Carly and Shani on your side.

"What do you mean, you're not coming?" Carly stared at Gillian, who had pushed aside her physics textbooks and set her chin in her hands as she watched me collect my bag and locate a sweater in case the fog came in later.

"If I don't get my homework out of the way this afternoon, I can't tutor Kaz in the morning. If he doesn't get some help, he flunks his physics test on Monday. It's kind of like nuclear fission. A chain reaction producing an explosion at the end."

"Or an implosion," Shani put in. "Come on, girl. You need a break."

"She's been studying practically nonstop all week." I

surfaced triumphantly from the wardrobe with a cashmere sweater as light as a puff of tropical air. "It'll be fun, Gillian. And it's Friday night. Even if you don't find a dress, we can still go for supper and a movie."

For a moment, I thought she'd waver and give in. Then she looked at the pile of books. "I really want to, but I have to prioritize. Homework first."

"Can't Kaz find help closer to home? What's Danyel doing?" He probably had as much of a struggle with physics as Kaz did, but two heads were always better than one.

"Bio," Shani said. "Not so helpful on the physics side." Shani gazed at Gillian with a mix of pity and admiration. "You're a better woman than I am."

"No," Gillian said bleakly. "I just have a heavier load this term than you do."

Once she made up her mind, I knew there was no changing it. "Can we bring you something, at least? Popcorn? Printer cartridges? Red Bull?"

Gillian shook her head. "I'm good. Once I get through this pile, I'll feel better about it. I'd rather do it now than ruin Sunday with it."

She had a point.

"It's not the same without all of us together," Carly grumbled on the way downtown on the train. It was lucky for our social lives that San Francisco had such a great transit system. This place is like New York—people can go all their lives without owning a car. Spencer doesn't allow student cars on campus anyway, so even if a person did have hers here, there was nowhere to put it. "No fair that she has to stay behind."

"You know how she is." I hung onto the metal pole next to their seat. "God first, school second, fun last."

"As opposed to us, who scramble it up any which way," Shani said.

"At least the second two," Carly reminded her. "Mess with the first one at your own risk."

Shani laughed and acknowledged the truth of that. "Not that I'm changing the subject or anything, but how weird is it that Emily Overton wanted to come with us today?"

"She did?" She hadn't said a word since she'd run out on me at lunch. We got off the train at the Montgomery station and headed through the double doors into the massive food court and the escalator that would take us into San Francisco Centre. "She was talking weird in the dining room, that's for sure. Wanted to know whether I would rat on someone if they had some kind of moral problem."

"What?" Carly made a confused face at me over her shoulder as we rode the escalator up.

"It's a mystery. Then Vanessa came by and snarked at her, and she ran away."

"Girl's off her meds," Shani said.

"Maybe, but she's also hooked in to what's going on at school. Must be some scandal brewing."

"There's always a scandal brewing with Vanessa's crowd, whether she's speaking to them or not. She creates them just for her own amusement." Carly led us into Nordstrom. "Ooh, check out the new Rag and Bone leather jacket."

Looking at clothes was much more fun than wondering what was up with Emily. When we finished with the mall, we walked up Post to Union Square, where Macy's, Saks, and Neiman Marcus held down three of its four corners like the *grandes dames* they were.

"I'm heading over to Britex to find some fabric," Carly told us. "Meet you here on the steps at five thirty?"

"You know, it's so much easier just to buy a dress." Shani folded her arms and stuck out a hip.

"I have a rep to uphold," Carly told her, nose in the air with *faux* snootiness. "Everything I make goes into my portfolio."

"You don't need a portfolio now," I said. "You already got into both schools you wanted."

"There is life after college. I'll need samples of everything I've done when I'm interviewing in costume departments in Hollywood and with designers."

"Man." I glanced at Shani. "How did I wind up with you guys as friends? All of you have everything so planned out. I feel like a doofus. Or like the grasshopper in that fable."

Carly slipped an arm around my waist and gave me a squeeze. "Some people figure out the talents God gave them early. With other people it takes more time. Besides, no doofus ever short-listed for the Hearst Medal."

"Point taken. Okay, see you right here at five thirty." I glanced at Shani. "Come on. We're on a mission."

But even as we filled dressing room after dressing room with beautiful dresses, it kept nagging at me—how they all knew what they wanted to do and I . . . didn't. Don't get me wrong. When you're seventeen, who really knows these things for sure? People change, circumstances change, you go from school to college to who knows where. Life is change, and you put your trust in God that He knows what He's doing.

But I guess what was bothering me most was that my friends had a handle on their talent and I didn't. I mean, look at Carly. Most people look at five yards of blue chiffon and see five yards of blue chiffon. Carly doesn't. She sees a Grecian draped sleeve and a high waist and a flowing skirt cut in a fishtail train. And Shani? Well, though they're night and day to look at, she and Mac are sisters under the skin, which is probably why they're always e-mailing each other. They're career girls from the word go, and graduation isn't so much something to work for as an annoyance to kick out of the way on the road to bigger and better things.

Even Gillian knows her talent. Talents. She may not know which of them to pick or what school will help her channel them the best, but she knows she has them.

And what do I have?

I don't have a Hearst Medal, despite what Carly said. It was great to be a finalist, but who ever remembers the person who came in second? Other than the admissions people at UCSB, which was good, okay, I get that. But who else?

I rest my case.

The Valentino babydoll I'd just tried on made me look fat. Who came up with the dumb idea that bubble hems were cute? They made everyone look fat. I tore it off and hung it up with the rest of the colorful plunder hanging on the back of the door. Clearly I was not destined to find a dress today.

I knocked on Shani's dressing-room door. "How are you doing?"

She opened it in a sleek LBD with crystal beading all over the bodice. "I don't know why I'm torturing myself. I know I'm not going to buy anything."

"It's your Cotillion dress, Shani. It's once in a lifetime."

"You say that about every school event you get a new dress for."

"But graduation really is only once in a lifetime. And you've got two mil—"

"Shh!"

"Well, you do. You can afford one dress."

She shook her head and closed the door. Behind it, I heard the mosquito shriek of a zipper. "Nope. I'll wear the Lagerfeld. No one will have seen it since the premiere of *The Middle Window*, and who cares if the fashion sites make snide remarks? I'll be on my way to Cambridge, Mass."

"I hope not. I hope you guys will take at least a week and come and stay with me like last summer."

Clothes rustled, and then she opened the door again, back in her street look. "That's a deal, girlfriend."

I may not be able to count on myself to know what I'm doing, but I know I can count on my friends.

NORMALLY, IF WE weren't shopping, the girls and I would do something fun together on the weekend, like go down to the beach or get a ride up to Napa to hang out with Brett's family at their vineyard. But Gillian's work ethic seemed to have infected Carly, too, and when I couldn't even convince Shani to go over to Telegraph Hill on Saturday to grab a coffee and watch the wild parrots, I gave up.

Resigning myself to homework, I pulled on a comfy denim mini, a (sloganless, per school rules) T-shirt, and flip-flops and drifted down to the library. May as well start on my English paper. Technically, I could have waived English in my final term of senior year, but I liked it. Papers were interesting, and in this class, The World of Jane Austen, what was not to like? My paper compared *Sense and Sensibility* with Elizabeth Gaskell's *Wives and Daughters*. All I needed was some literary criticism and some feminist theory to back up my arguments, and I'd be good to go.

I cruised the stacks, happily debating the merits of books with interesting titles like *Diversionary Tactics: Feminine Au-*

thority in the Novels of Burney and Austen and *A Galaxy of Disagreeable Women*, when I turned a corner and nearly tripped over Emily, who was sitting on the hardwood floor.

"Watch it!"

"Sorry." I grabbed for the stack of books teetering beside her before it fell over. "You need a cart."

"Nah. I only want one of these. It's picking the right one that's the hard part."

I couldn't remember ever seeing her looking at a book in public. This was a rare sighting. "I didn't think you were into studying."

She gave me a glance that was this close to an eye roll. "I still have to pass Senior Lit. Besides, it's not like I have anything else to do."

I wasn't touching that one. The girl needed some new friends and some inspiration, in that order. Much as she exasperated me sometimes, there was a vulnerability about her that made me want to reach out to her. It was this same vulnerability that got her picked on by people like Rory Stapleton. Which, in my opinion, was all the more reason to reach out.

"I'm looking for some backup for my paper, too." I glanced over the spines above her, my head tilted to read the titles.

"Lissa, have you thought any more about what we talked about before?"

I straightened. "We didn't really talk about anything. If something's bugging you, just spit it out and help me understand how I can help, okay?"

She looked both ways down the rows of shelving, though there was no one in this section but us. Mrs. Lynn, the librarian, wasn't on duty on the weekend, and the circulation people stayed behind the desk. "That's the problem. I want to spit it out, but I don't know who to tell."

"Your moral problem," I prompted. Not that I really wanted to know, especially if it were some A-list drama. But she clearly needed to get it off her chest.

"Not mine!"

"Okay. *The* moral problem."

"It's just that somebody's done something that's going to come out, like, any day now. She's trying to hide it, and personally, I don't think she should even be allowed to stay here."

"A friend of yours?"

Now I did get an eye roll. "Maybe once. Not now."

"So . . . you want to know if you should tell someone? So this person will be expelled?"

"No-o-o." She made me sound hopelessly stupid for not getting it. "The person needs help. But of course she won't ask for it. And I'm afraid the—someone will get hurt."

"Did they forget their appointment with their therapist and they're out of control, or what?" I couldn't think of anyone who fit that description, unless you counted Rory Stapleton.

"Urgghh!" Emily jerked her backpack off the floor and stood. "That is so like you. You don't understand something, so you make smart remarks instead of helping."

I blinked. "I was serious. Call me blond, but I don't know how to help if I don't get—"

"Forget it." She left her stack of books where they were and stalked off down the corridor between the stacks.

"Okay," I said blankly. Then I pushed at her pile with my toes. Ooh, look at that. *Reader, I Married Him: A Study of the Women Characters of Jane Austen, Charlotte Bronte, Elizabeth Gaskell and George Eliot.* "Thanks." I tucked the book under my arm.

Back in our room, Gillian took a break from equations and listened to my summary of the situation. "Sounds to me like she's just looking for attention," she said finally. "If there was something going on that meant danger to someone, we'd have heard about it."

"Not necessarily. Look how long it took us to figure out who was selling the exam answers last year."

"Don't remind me. But that wasn't physical danger, which is what Emily meant, right? It's some kind of moral thing?"

I nodded. "I'm missing the connection between that and someone getting hurt, which is the part she won't tell me. You're probably right. So. When does the *Coaching with Kaz* show start?"

She glanced at the clock on her monitor. "Ten. I didn't think he'd be awake, but that's what he said."

"Desperation will push a man to extremes."

"Luckily we both have iChat, and I can point him to a research site while I talk him through it."

"Can I talk to him when you're done?"

"Sure."

I got to work blocking out my paper—and blocking out the sound of two agonizing hours of physics coaching. When at last Gillian got up from her desk and waved me over, the first thing I saw on her screen was the top of Kaz's shaggy head. He lay facedown on the desk.

"Yo, Kaz," I said. "Are you alive?"

"Barely." When he lifted his head, his eyes were bleary. "She hurt my brain."

From the bathroom, Gillian snorted. "It's good for you. Think how much less painful the exam will be."

"I wish you were here," he told me pathetically. "You could rub my head."

"You can pay people for that, you know."

"It's not the same as when you do it." He blinked and started to come back to life. "Whatcha up to?"

"English paper. Very fun. Comparing the expectations of the marriageable girl in Jane Austen versus Elizabeth Gaskell."

"You call that fun?"

"Sure. Basically I get to write a paper about dating. It just doesn't get better than that."

"Right, because you're the expert."

"I've had some experience," I said primly. Which he knew all about, the ratball. "What about you? Prom's coming up, the weekend before ours. Who are you going to ask?"

"I probably won't even go. What about you?"

"They call it Senior Cotillion here. It's on June eighteenth. Danyel is coming to take Shani, so it'd be fun if you rode along."

"Uh, did you just ask me to prom?"

"I guess so. If you didn't have other plans that weekend."

Chin in hand, Kaz gazed at me. "You really have a way of making a guy feel special."

"What, did you want a bouquet of roses by FedEx?" I grinned at him.

"No."

"Well, what then?"

He shook his head. "Never mind. Gotta go. Me and Danyel are gonna shake the cobwebs out at the beach."

"Ride one for me." I tried not to sound wistful as I signed off. "Hope you feel better."

Why was everyone so cranky today? Was it something I said?

chapter 5

ON SUNDAY, the pastor at the little clapboard church in Marin talked about waiting on God's timing, which made Gillian and me glance at each other and smile. Okay, it was clear the Lord was listening to our nagging. It was just a matter of waiting for His answer.

I was still thinking about this as I walked down the corridor on Monday, on the way to horrible disgusting Chemistry. It was better to reflect on things that made my eternal soul happy because it was a fact that nothing I did would make the Chem instructor, Mr. Milsom, happy.

The long, wood-panelled corridors had terrible acoustics, which is why the unusual noise level finally penetrated my abstraction by the time I got to the sciences wing. Clumps of students whispered together, and I tuned in to snatches of conversation as I passed.

". . . didn't think I'd ever see . . ."

". . . told me she was going to keep it."

". . . so good. She's going down, baby, and I'm the first one to dance on her grave."

Yikes. What was going on?

I dropped the glossy Kate Spade tote that held my books and laptop next to my lab stool, and nudged Jeremy, who was my lab partner. "Did something happen? What's everybody talking about?"

He gazed at me blankly. "Huh?"

He was such a guy. I looked around for someone who might be better informed. Aha. Summer Liang was on the Cotillion Committee and they knew everything. I gave her a smile. "Hey, Summer. What's up?"

To my surprise, she didn't make me work for it. "Haven't you heard?"

"A bunch of people are talking, but I haven't gotten the details."

"I can hardly believe it. In fact, I didn't believe it, but Emily Overton says it's true, and she would know."

Patience. "Know what?"

"That Vanessa Talbot is going to have a—"

"Miss Liang!" Summer jumped about a foot as Mr. Milsom strode into the room. "I trust your remarks concern the formulae I have on the board? Pop quiz, people. Notebooks away, pencils out."

"Urgghhh!" My frustration level spiked. Did the man not know better than to interrupt a conversation? Especially when it involved some kind of scandal starring none other than my nemesis?

As I copied down the formulas, my fingers gripped the pencil so hard I was sure I'd break it. How was I going to get the rest of that sentence out of Summer? Too bad my phone would get confiscated the moment I pulled it out to send her a discreet text. Could I pass her a note? No, that would get confiscated, too.

Why had I never learned Morse code? Or ASL?

I handed in my poor excuse for a quiz. Good thing my grades in my other classes were so good—they'd make up for this one. How could a person think of chemical formulas when something huge was going down?

Don't think I'm a hound for being so anxious to lap up the gossip. But can you blame me? Between Emily's dire hints and the level of tension in the air, something was wrong and I wanted to know what it was. After all, Emily had said someone was in danger, hadn't she?

In the ten-minute break between Chem and Lab, my luck finally changed.

TEXT MESSAGE

To: BFFs
From: Carly Aragon
          3rd floor girls bathroom, stat.

I was already halfway there. Gillian just beat me to the door, and we found Carly and Shani inside the wheelchair stall.

"Somebody please give me the scoop," I begged. "I can't stand it."

"Stand what?" Gillian wanted to know. "This better be fast, Carly. I've got a rehearsal with the school orchestra in, like, four minutes."

"So none of you have heard," Carly whispered, looking from one of us to the next.

"No, and if you have, spit it out," I begged.

Our gazes were all riveted on her face, with its huge brown eyes. "I heard it last period and I still can't believe it." She took a breath. "Vanessa Talbot is pregnant."

"No," Gillian breathed.

"Impossible," Shani said.

I couldn't speak. Shock had frozen every thought but one: What would happen to Vanessa now?

THE NEWS ROCKETED through the entire school with the velocity of a nuclear blast. By the end of the last period that morning, I think even the janitors and the laundry service had heard. Only the most benighted of the computer science geeks, who only talked among themselves in incomprehensible syllables anyway, went about their business as if they'd never heard of Vanessa Talbot.

Come to think of it, they probably hadn't.

The only thing that got me through the Lab period that followed Chem was the sharp end of Jeremy's elbow, which kept digging into my ribs every time I went off into a daze.

Vanessa. Having a baby. No wonder Emily didn't know who to tell. Guess she doesn't have to worry about that now. Moral problem. Wow. But what did she mean about danger to someone? The baby? Or someone else?

"Ow!"

"I asked you, how many grams of solution?"

I stared at the beaker he had ready for me. How could he possibly think of grams of solution at a time like this?

When I finally escaped and ran down to the dining room at lunch, I found the rest of the girls and Brett already there.

"I can't believe she kept it a secret this long," Shani said, digging into her risotto. "I mean, how many months along is she?"

Carly salted her own risotto and handed the shaker to Brett. "I heard it happened during Christmas vacation. In Italy."

I leaned toward her. "Who's the father?"

Brett answered me, much to my surprise. "Rumor says it was one of the gardeners."

Shani's eyes held doubt. "Vanessa and a gardener? I'm thinking not." Then she inhaled, as if an idea had just slapped her upside the head. "You don't think it was—it couldn't have been—" She stopped.

Gillian shook her head so emphatically her hair swung. "No. No way. Not Rashid. They broke up in the middle of December, before vacation started."

"What difference does a week or two make?"

"A big difference if you're talking about the heir to the Lion Throne. Look at it this way." Gillian pointed her fork at Shani. "If there was even a breath of suspicion it was Rashid's, his parents would have sent the entire Yasiri Secret Service to extract the truth by any means necessary, two months ago."

Shani sat back and let her breath out. "You're right. If they could send their agents to hunt me down in Scotland about a viral video, they'd for sure send them here about a baby."

"Not to mention Vanessa would make sure she had her hands well and truly on the Star of the Desert," I pointed out. "The girl does like her bling."

"That's a high price to pay," Brett said quietly. "Even for—"

The door opened and Vanessa walked in. I tried not to

look. I really did. But as she took her plate of risotto and walked over to the juice bar to get a drink, it seemed like every eye in the dining room was fixed on her.

Or more precisely, on her stomach.

From the back, she looked the same as any of us. Plaid skirt, white blouse, blue cardigan. But were her feet in their Prada flats planted further apart than usual? Had her walk changed? When did a person's hips start spreading? I tried to remember whether they'd covered that in freshman Life Sciences.

When she turned with her plate held protectively close to her stomach, her profile told it all. Even the cardigan couldn't hide the little bump or the fact that she'd had to switch to a skirt with an elastic waistband, like the ones Emily wore.

I bet that galled her.

Five months pregnant. Wow.

"I can't believe I didn't see it before," I breathed. "I mean, Apple Bottoms are one thing. But this?"

"I can't either, with your obsession with her," Gillian said.

"I'm not obsessed," I protested for about the sixty-fifth time in two years. "It's just self-preservation."

Carrying her plate and her iced smoothie, Vanessa strolled toward the table in the window. Her body looked relaxed and her eyelids drooped in their usual "I'm bored out of my skull" expression. You had to hand it to her. If it had been me in that predicament—which it wouldn't be, considering the promise I made to God—I'm sure I would have been slinking around, hoping no one would look at me. Or I'd have paid someone to collect a tray and bring it to my room. Or better yet, I'd have chosen to be home-schooled.

I'm sure she knew the news was out. But other people's opinions had never been important to her before. Why should things be different now?

DeLayne Geary put her plate down on the table in the window, with her back to the sun. Before Vanessa could reach it herself, Christine Powell, Rory Stapleton, and three other people who had been hanging out with that group lately materialized with their trays and sat down. Vanessa walked over, skewered DeLayne with her gaze, and waited.

And waited.

"Excuse me, D. You know that's my seat."

DeLayne glanced at Christine as the buzz of chatter at the tables around them dropped a couple of notches. People tuned into the drama as avidly as if it were a reality show. "There's no room here for skanks."

The words dropped like a stone and silence spread out in rings of shock and breathless anticipation.

Vanessa didn't even blink. "In that case, I'll ask Christine and Rory to move. I know what the two of you were up to in the boys' shower after soccer practice."

Ewww. Don't make me look at that image. As Carly would say, it makes my eyes bleed.

"At least I wasn't stupid enough to get knocked up," Christine retorted, her mouth curled with scorn.

"We don't hang out with stupid people," DeLayne said. "So you'll have to find somewhere else to sit."

"Don't make me destroy you," Vanessa said quietly. "You know what I know."

DeLayne's jaw hardened and she narrowed her eyes. "What? That there were two people there and one is just as guilty as the other?"

"But one doesn't have the proof the other does."

"Maybe one has more cred than the other. Now." She raked Vanessa from top to bottom with a scornful gaze. "So go ahead, skank. Tell your little story. See who comes out looking the worst."

For a moment neither one backed down, and animosity crackled in the air between them. But possession is nine-tenths of the law, and DeLayne wasn't moving her rear from that chair for anything. I had no idea what secret they were holding over each other's heads, but DeLayne clearly had a handle on the concept of "moral superiority," and wasn't afraid to wield it the way Kaz's avatars use their swords when he plays *World of Warcraft*. Totally without mercy.

"PeeGee," I heard someone whisper at the next table. "PeeGee Princess!"

The whole table took up the chant. "PeeGee Princess! PeeGee Princess!"

Now the whole dining room got into the beat. "PeeGee Princess!" Some guy used his fork against his tray, the table, and his plate to work out a backbeat. "PeeGee Princess, she's a skank!"

Vanessa pursed her flawlessly glossed lips and rolled her eyes as if she were surrounded by a room full of un-ruly kindergarteners. Then she turned lazily on her heel and walked out the door with her plate and her rapidly melting smoothie, leaving the dining room in an uproar of laughter and jeers.

Our table was one of the few that were still quiet. We glanced at each other, unsure of what to say. Brett shook his head and shoveled food into his mouth.

Shani took a bite of her risotto, watching as some fool across the room mimed walking with a pregnant stomach, knees bent and spine arched, repeating "PeeGee Princess" as if he'd just that moment thought of it, and sitting down in a gale of laughter.

"I always wondered if Vanessa started that little rumor about me in the fall," she said quietly. "That's what they called me, you know, all those nasties in her group."

The irony was not lost on any of us.

Gillian leaned back and caught my eye over Jeremy's shoulder. "How low the mighty are fallen," she said.

"It's not over yet," I told her. "Not even close."

Most of the time I enjoy being right. But not then.

....

✉

To: hrhr@gulftel.yz
From: shanna@spenceracad.edu
Date: May 10, 2010
Re: Question

Hi Rashid,

I've been sitting here for an hour trying to get up the courage to ask you this. Carly thinks I'm researching a paper, but I can't think or talk or function until I know, and you're the only person I can ask.

I don't know if you've heard, but a big scandal broke today. Vanessa Talbot is pregnant—about five months along. And now that I've said that, I guess I'd better say the rest of it.

Is there any chance the baby could be yours? I know it's none of my business. You have every right to be angry that I would even ask this. But I hope that once you get over my rudeness, you'll remember we're good friends. I want to respect and think the best of my friends.

Love, Shani

....

chapter 6

MOST SCHOOL SCANDALS are a nine-day wonder, gaped at and then forgotten because the person gets expelled. But this . . . it was more like a nine-month wonder. You couldn't exactly expel a person for expecting a baby, could you? I mean, technically it's not a crime.

It's a whole lot of other things, but not a crime.

That evening at dinner, Vanessa didn't show up, so De-Layne and Christine and Emily—she must have thought it was safe to come out of the bushes—sat at the table in the window, pretending it had been theirs all along. Emily even came over and invited me to sit with them.

"Is that what you wanted to talk to me about on the weekend?" I asked her in a low voice. "About Vanessa?"

She nodded. "It doesn't matter now."

"But you said there was danger. Did you mean to the baby?"

"Sure." She glanced behind me, as if to make sure Gillian and Carly were out of earshot. "If she gets an abortion."

My stomach turned over. "It's a little late for that, isn't it?" My knowledge on that subject was about the same as my knowledge of astronomy: minimal. But now that it had come up, Vanessa certainly could have taken a step like that the second she'd seen the pink line on the pregnancy test. I am totally against such a step, mind you. Just the thought of it makes me ill. But Vanessa? How could anyone know what was in that girl's heart?

"Not the way she's talking."

That didn't sound good. "Emily, did you break the story?"

She blinked innocent eyes at me. "It would have broken anyway. It's not like you can hide something like that. Sure you don't want to eat with us? I'm saving you a chair."

"That's okay. Maybe tomorrow."

"Whatever."

I sat next to Carly and exhaled as if I'd been holding my breath. "Weirdness."

"Of course she broke the story," Carly said. "Vanessa treats her like last week's trash. I'm only surprised it didn't happen a month ago. Or the week we started school."

"She wasn't showing then." Why would Vanessa risk everything by staying pregnant? Did Emily's hints from before mean she still planned to get an abortion at this late stage? My blood seemed to thicken with cold at the awful thought.

"Can we talk about something else?" Gillian asked around a spoonful of miso soup. "This subject is getting all the air time."

She was right. We could talk the topic to death, but there was nothing we could do about it. In the end, any decisions were up to Vanessa.

But still . . .

On Tuesday morning during free period, I tucked my Bible in my tote and instead of working on my Austen/Gaskell paper, headed outside. The marine layer that usually kept things cool in the summer was being held offshore by the wind from inland, which meant it was sunny and warm out on the lawn. Behind the music wing, the ground fell away in a slope of grass down to the street, and on a morning like today, you could catch some rays there.

Sitting at the top of the slope, my legs stretched out, I pulled my Bible out and began to read the poetry of Isaiah to calm my jangled spirit. Vanessa's life was no deal of mine. She'd made her choices and now she had to live with them, like anyone else. I pushed Emily's offhand remark about abortion out of my head. Not my choice. Not my business.

Two chapters later, someone walked up beside me, throwing the words of the prophet into shadow. I shaded my eyes with one hand and looked up.

"Hi, Lissa." Ashley Polk dropped her backpack on the grass. "Do you have a minute to talk?"

I'd worked with her on the Benefactors' Day Ball when I was a junior and she was the only sophomore on the committee. Other than that, our paths didn't cross much. I closed the Bible and tucked it into my tote.

"Is that a Bible?"

I nodded. "What can I do for you?"

"Do you always read it out in public like this?"

There had been a time when I would have said no. When the subject would not even have come up, because said book would have been stashed in a drawer in my room, never to see the light of public scrutiny or trigger potentially embarrassing questions about my faith.

After what my friends and I have been through, I've learned that faith is something to celebrate and be thankful for, not hide. If somebody can't handle that, it's their problem, not mine.

"Not always," I told her. "Just this morning. What's up?"

She folded herself onto the grass next to me, stretching out her strong soccer-player's legs. "I suppose you've heard about Vanessa Talbot and her little . . . problem."

Was this the conversation starter *du jour*? Did nobody comment on the weather anymore? "Uh-huh."

"The thing is, her problem is making a problem for us. The Cotillion Committee."

"Really?"

"Well, obviously."

I could feel stupid all on my own. I didn't need other people to help me along. "It may be obvious to you, but it's not to me." I reached for my tote. "Excuse me. I wasn't finished with my chapter."

"Lissa." She touched my wrist lightly with her fingers, her big blue eyes pleading. "I'm sorry. You're right. I'm just really stressed right now. I—we—the committee delegated me to ask for your help."

This was the last thing I'd expected. "What?"

"Vanessa is our consulting senior, right? She's the one who makes all the announcements, tells us what needs to be done, forms the subcommittees, delegates the P.R., all that stuff." When I nodded, she went on, "So how is it going to look on the night of the Cotillion when she's up there on that stage, big as a house?"

"Um . . ."

"The media and all the benefactor bigwigs, not to mention the board of regents and their wives, are all going to be there. What are they going to think if our mistress of ceremonies, the girl who's supposed to represent the senior class, is standing up there in her maternity dress, pregnant by some Italian gardener?"

"I think that's just a rumor," I managed to say.

"I don't care if it is. The point is, she's going to make us all look stupid and low-rent. And that is not what Spencer is about."

"Ashley, Vanessa is definitely not low-rent. And you know John Galliano is probably going to design her maternity clothes himself. She'll wind up restarting the rage for bubble dresses just when they were going out."

It looked as if it hurt her to smile. "Regardless, we're asking her to step down today. We're considering a small number of people who could take her place as senior consultant. Are you interested?"

"Me?!" I fell back on my hands. My elbows felt as if they would barely hold me up.

"You've got the experience," she said rapidly, as if to head my objections off at the pass. "You worked on the Benefactors' Day Ball and also Design Your Dreams last year. You're connected. And everyone knows you've got style."

That was nice to know. *Don't fall for flattery. Tell her no.* "I, uh . . ."

"At least think about it," Ashley begged.

"What about DeLayne? Or Emily, or someone in Vanessa's group?"

"We don't want a Vanessa clone," she replied with honesty as brutal as Gillian's. Only unlike Gillian's, it wasn't tempered with kindness. "We want someone different. Someone everybody likes. Someone who's dependable."

"Someone who's not likely to turn up pregnant."

"Exactly. There are only two or three people in the senior class who fit that description. And you're one of them."

Okay, I'd been sort of kidding. Yikes. These people were serious to the point of grimness about their Cotillion. Could I handle that? "When do you need my answer?"

"By Thursday at the latest, so we can vote on the short list. Our next meeting is on Friday, right after lunch. If you're the successful candidate, I can brief you on everything we've done, introduce you formally, and you can hit the ground running the same day."

My mother, charity benefit organizer extraordinaire, would really like this girl. I wondered if Ashley was interested in interning this summer. I also wondered who else was on the short list.

"I'll let you know by Wednesday," I said. "I have to talk—er, think it over first."

"We'd really appreciate it, Lissa." She climbed to her feet and picked up her backpack. "Personally, I'm lobbying for you. I think you'd be perfect for the job."

Which job—running the Cotillion Committee, or stepping into Vanessa's shoes? Because it was an unspoken fact that the most popular girl in the senior class was picked to be the senior consultant.

So what exactly did that make me?

WE HAD PRAYER circle that same night, but I didn't bring up Ashley's request there. I didn't want to trifle with the Lord's attention—and there were bigger problems to pray over. A couple of people lifted up Gillian and her decision about colleges. She prayed for her brother, the gymnast, who was getting ready for the Olympics. And me?

I thought I was going to pray for Gillian, too. But it's funny how the heart can take over when the brain is looking in the other direction.

"Father, this is probably going to surprise You, but I want to lift up Vanessa Talbot to You tonight. It's none of my business, but all of us are Your business. If she's thinking about, um, ending her pregnancy, I hope You'll help her change her mind and point out whatever path is in Your will for her. Even if she doesn't know it. In Jesus' name, amen."

People murmured "amen" and a little silence fell, as if they were digesting what I'd said. Finally, Shani flipped open her laptop and started Danyel's weekly video. I concentrated on his musical voice, lifting us all up as if he were right there with us, and tried to relax.

Afterward, Jeremy and Brett said they had other stuff to do and headed off. Shani and Gillian waited until we were out on the street, walking down to Starbucks. "So what's with the prayer, girlfriend?" Shani wanted to know. "I never expected to hear *that* name coming out of our circle, that's for sure."

"Why not? She can pray for whomever she wants," Carly said. "Ease up."

"I never said she couldn't," Shani retorted. "I just want to know what brought it on, is all."

"I don't know," I said. "It just—came out."

"I agree with Carly that a person should pray for someone if they're led to. Especially when it's over something as huge as an abortion. You can bet I'll be praying about that. But—" Gillian paused. "You know how Vanessa is. She's not the most trustworthy person on the planet, and I'd hate to see you get pulled into her orbit and have her find some way to hurt you."

I never expected a simple prayer to make my girls react like this. "I'm sure she has other things to think about." I shrugged. "I brought it to God. My work is done."

"Vanessa wouldn't thank you for it," Shani said quietly.

"There's another thing she won't thank me for." We pushed open the door and while we stood in line, I filled them in on the Cotillion Committee's leadership problems.

Carly took her mocha and led the way to a table in the corner. "Yeah, they asked me, too." She shook her head. "Even though my only qualification is who I'm dating. I think you should do it," she said to me. "It seems like a no-brainer."

"What about you?"

Carly shook her head. "Organizing events isn't my thing. Going to them is way more fun."

"You guys know what it means, right? Vanessa will never forgive me." I took a sip of my honey latte.

"Why should that bother you?" Gillian wanted to know. "She hasn't forgiven you yet just for being alive."

True enough. "I guess I'm still hearing them laugh at her in the dining room today. It's so ugly."

"We weren't laughing," Shani pointed out.

"I know. But I'm not sure about jumping on the bandwagon and adding more ugly to it, you know?"

"How is being the senior consultant adding to it?" Carly asked. "Someone has to do it. You're good at that kind of thing. It may as well be you."

"I am?"

"Ashley told you herself that she noticed what you did for those other events."

Could a person build a career on a knack for event planning? Maybe she could. At least it was something to put on the plus side of my very short list of talents. I might not be a fashion designer or a piano prodigy, but I could pull together a few hundred people and entertain them.

"Vanessa's not going to take it out on you," Carly said. "She's got bigger things to think about. No pun intended."

But in that Carly proved to be wrong. On Wednesday, I left core class and headed upstairs to second period, still trying to figure out whether or not I should text Ashley and tell her yes. Vanessa came out of the language lab and practically hip-checked me into a row of lockers.

"Well, if it isn't the new senior consultant." Her dark eyes were smudged with shadow. Hadn't she slept? Or had she just been a little heavy-handed with the color palette this morning? "You back-stabbing hag."

Hold your ground. You've got nowhere to go but backward. "The committee hasn't voted. And I haven't decided if I even want to do it."

"Luckily for you, it doesn't take a brain to make that decision."

My cheeks flushed hot, then paled. "I obviously take it more seriously than you do. And you don't need to get personal about it."

"Oh, it's personal." She leaned in, eyes snapping, while I tried to keep my spine straight and not give her an inch. "Those stupid cows don't know a good leader when they have one. But I guess they'll find out, won't they?"

Ten different nasty cracks hovered on the tip of my tongue and I hung onto my self-control with both hands. I would not become like her. Turning into the blond version of Vanessa Talbot was not the summit of my ambition for the school year.

But deep inside, I knew it was possible. I could crush her

with one nasty line. I could face down DeLayne Geary, and soon that group would be giving up their chairs for me at the table in the window. I could be the one deciding who was cool and who was outcast. I could have my pick of dates for the Cotillion.

Oh, yeah. With my longtime nemesis out of the way, I could have everything I once thought I'd wanted. Now there was a frightening thought: Anakin Skywalker turning into Darth Vader, right here at Spencer Academy.

"I have nothing to do with the committee's decision, Vanessa."

"Like I'm going to believe that. I heard you were talking to Ashley yesterday."

"She asked me if I was interested, that's all. They're asking a bunch of people."

"Witch. I know what you want."

"Really?" I almost laughed. "How can you? I haven't even figured that out yet."

"Freaking Bible-thumper. They'll see what a Judas you are."

Okay, turning the other cheek has its limits. "Vanessa. For the last time, I didn't ask for the job. They offered. If you don't like it, you shouldn't have—" I stopped and glanced at her stomach.

Her hand twitched, as if she'd barely restrained herself from slapping me. And then she turned on her heel and stalked away down the corridor, leaving me feeling sick and shaken as I made my way to the history classroom.

Vanessa 0. Lissa 0.

....

✉

To: shanna@spenceracad.edu
From: hrhr@gulftel.yz
Date: May 12, 2010
Re: Re: Question

My friend,

It's fortunate there is an understanding between us. Had my father seen your e-mail, I am sure he would have provoked an Incident. As it is, I deleted it from my mail and the palace server before the Secret Service found it. You see, my tutoring in computer science at Stanford has its uses after all. :)

The answer to your question is no. My relationship with Vanessa, such as it was, did not progress to the point you fear. I understand my duty, and it does not include foolish behavior. Not that I didn't want to, you understand. But if I were going to take such a step, it would be with someone willing to accept the Star of the Desert and all that it means.

I still regret that you did not, but on the other hand, I am rewarded with a friend I can count on no matter the circumstances.

Be at peace, Shani. I hope you are well. Please delete this when you have read it.

Rashid

....

chapter 7

POPULARITY IS LIKE a storm front. A bunch of seemingly unrelated factors like pressure and movement and small changes all come together, and before you know it, the atmosphere is completely different. You either hide from it, fight it, or go with it.

That week, the social weather vane at Spencer swung in one direction after another, looking for somewhere to point. Carly, who had rock-solid status as the girlfriend of our school's most popular guy, and who, after the Design Your Dreams extravaganza last year, had outshone most of the girls on talent alone, chose to hide. In other words, she told the Cotillion Committee no, thanks. She simply didn't care about being popular. What mattered to her were her family, her friends, and Brett, in pretty much that order.

DeLayne Geary fought for it. But you know how you can sense desperation in a girl who really wants a boyfriend? It's in the intensity of her stare, the hilarity of her laugh, and the way she moves. DeLayne was like that—just a little too much of everything. In the end, it netted her zip.

And then there was me. I went to class, did my assignments, and hung out with my friends, avoiding run-ins with Vanessa whenever necessary. Pretty much what I'd been doing for two years, right? But between the time I told the Cotillion Committee I was interested and Thursday at lights-out, when Ashley texted me to say they'd voted for me unanimously, even I could see which way the wind blew.

It was behind my back, pushing me gently but inexorably into the limelight.

"Congratulations." Gillian gave me a brief, absentminded hug and went to bed. I mean, I know stuff like this doesn't really register on her personal Richter scale, but she could have been a *little* happier about it.

Carly's hug the next morning made up for it, though. She squeezed me with delight and practically tap-danced. "I knew they'd vote you in," she said. "You're the only person who could do it."

"Do you know who the others were?"

"DeLayne and Christine."

"Oh." Ashley had told me they weren't considering De-Layne. Somehow I was really glad I hadn't lost to her.

"I'm glad you beat out DeLayne," Shani told me. Was the girl psychic or what? "She'd have been unbearable. Your committee needs to be led, not bossed around."

My committee. I liked the sound of that.

Ashley had asked me to meet her in the dining room for breakfast and a briefing before the committee meeting at two. Even though we were a little early, Emily still beat us to the window table, where she sat sipping a cappuccino.

She waved me into the middle chair. "I saved you a seat."

"Thanks." Shani and Carly took the end seats while I hung

my tote over the back of the chair where Vanessa used to sit. "This feels weird. DeLayne is going to have kittens."

"Don't let anyone else hear you say that. You don't want to show fear, or DeLayne will stage a coup with you like she did with Vanessa."

"Emily, I don't think—"

"Hi, Lissa." A group of seniors from my Austen class waved on their way to the juice bar. Derrik Vaughan, who was the soccer team's star goalie and who had come once with Brett to prayer circle, caught my eye and smiled from across the room. Christine Powell put her stuff down one table away and paused next to ours. "Hi, Lissa. Congratulations on your nomination. Can I get you something from the juice bar while I'm up?"

"No. Um, thanks." That was generous of her. "I'll wait."

"Just let me know."

"Okay, now I'm really feeling weird," I murmured.

"Welcome to the new regime." Emily licked the foam mustache off her upper lip.

"I am not a regime."

"You will be."

That definitely had Yoda-like echoes, and not in a good way. "I'm not afraid," Luke Skywalker had said to him. And then look what happened. Gulp.

Seeing Ashley making her way across the room, arms full of folders and a big white binder, was a relief. Here was something I could touch and see. Something real I could work with. Something concrete and weirdness-free.

We got our yogurt and fruit and I got a tall glass of watermelon juice, icy cold. I bit into a big boysenberry as Ashley opened her binder. "Here's what we have so far."

Guest lists, ticket sale projections, table arrangements,

caterer. So far, so good. Seating chart, yup. Band. "No band yet?"

"Not yet. The music committee is having a hard time with a booking."

"With all the great bands in town? Ashley, there's only, like, a month to go."

With a glance at Carly and Shani, who were keeping their conversation low so they didn't interrupt us, she leaned closer. "Vanessa was managing that herself. She didn't share her progress with us and we took it for granted she had it handled."

"Oh, boy." I sighed. "I'll talk to her and see where she was on it."

"Good luck with that." An unspoken *You'll need it* hung in the air between us.

No point in wasting time. "The committee meeting's at two, right? In your room?" Ashley nodded. "I'll find her, get a status, and meet you then."

"Are you sure you want to do that? We can just start from scratch, you know. Tinker Davis's dad owns a record label and a bunch of clubs. She's already said she can call in some favors."

I shook my head. "Vanessa might already have someone booked and is just holding out to make us come to her. I'm not proud. I'll do it."

My yogurt churned uneasily in my stomach as I climbed the stairs a few minutes later, smiling at people and returning greetings. Since when did everyone know my name? And they all said it correctly, too. The days of *Melissa* seemed to be gone forever. I guess I could be thankful for that.

Outside the door of Vanessa's room, I took a breath to settle myself, and knocked.

Silence.

Then I heard sounds of someone moving around. The toilet flushed, and then the door opened. Her face as white as an exam sheet, eyes huge and almost bruised-looking, Vanessa swayed in the doorway. The acrid scent of vomit wafted past me. "What?" She bit the end off the word.

"Are you okay?"

She rolled her eyes. "Does it look like it?"

"Do you have the flu?" I took a step back. The smell was awful, but even worse was the vulnerability in her face. It made an uncomfortable contrast with her tone, like she was forcing herself to keep up the usual attitude.

"What are you, School Nurse Barbie? I'm pregnant, you idiot. It happens."

"I thought that went away after the first couple of months."

"I'm a special case. What do you want?"

It took me a minute to remember why I was there, and why it was important. "I came by to check on the status of the band for the Cotillion."

She leaned on the doorjamb as if she needed something to hold her up. "There is no band. I stopped caring right about the time they voted you in."

"Uh. Okay." Another step back. "That's all I needed to know."

Without answering, she closed the door in my face, and I heard the sound of retching from inside.

I retreated down the corridor as fast as I could. Why on earth would anyone put herself through this? I mean, Vanessa and I have never been less than despised enemies, but this was enough to make even me feel sorry for her.

You're probably the only one.

True enough. With Dani gone, she had her room to herself, at least.

Which means there's no one to look after her.

She looked pretty bad. Probably hadn't been able to eat. And the baby would need food.

"Inasmuch as you do it unto the least of these my brethren, you do it unto me." That's what Jesus said. He probably didn't have this exact situation in mind, but His words still applied.

I glanced at the clock and headed back to the dining room. Fifteen minutes. That should be enough time. I located the kitchen manager and asked her what I would need. She filled a tray and I took it back to the first-floor dorm.

Vanessa opened up a little faster this time, and instead of the awful smell I dreaded, she smelled minty fresh. She'd just brushed her teeth.

"You again." Her gaze dropped to the tray.

"Consommé," I said. "Flat ginger ale. Crackers. Small bites at a time, Ms. Guccione says. It will help keep it down."

"Bite me." She began to swing the door shut, but I stuck my foot in the gap and forced my way past her. Since I was carrying a tray with an open bowl of hot broth, this was not easy, but all those years of battling waves have made me stronger than I look.

"Say what you want, but I'm leaving this here."

"Why?"

"Because the baby needs something to eat."

"Why do you care?"

No way would I tell her that she looked fragile enough to break. That it hurt me to feel the sharp edge of her scorn in a way that it never had before. "You should."

"Don't tell me what to do or how to feel." Eyes narrowed,

she looked ready to pick up the bowl and toss its contents in my face.

I wasn't taking any chances with her throwing arm. I'd seen her overhand serve on the volleyball team and you didn't mess with that. I closed the door behind me. And through it I heard, not the crash of cutlery on the back of the door, but the clink of the spoon against china.

Relief filled me.

Lissa 1, Vanessa 0.

"WHAT'S WITH GILLIAN?" I had caught up with Shani and Carly on their way to third-period Life Sciences, and Shani had spotted Gillian marching down the corridor, seemingly unaware we were there. "She seems kind of out of it."

They both looked at me. "No idea. This whole college thing is really bugging her."

"There's more to it than that," Carly said. "Is everything okay with her and Jeremy?"

"Just because a girl's got stuff on her mind doesn't mean it's boy related," I said.

"Ninety percent of the time it does," Shani told me with the maddening certainty of someone who had a boyfriend talking to someone who didn't.

"You guys would know," I said as if it totally didn't bother me. "But with Gillian, it's probably related to classes in one way or another."

"Speaking of boys," Shani said, "I got an answer from Rashid on a certain question."

Carly raised her eyebrows. "And the answer was?"

"No. He says their relationship wasn't like that."

I snorted. "According to Vanessa, they were Edward and Bella, part two."

"Edward and Bella never had sex before they were married," Carly reminded me. "So maybe she was right."

"I am so not having that picture in my head," Shani said firmly. "See you later, Lissa."

We parted ways in the corridor, Carly heading to Fashion Design, where she was a teaching assistant, Shani to Organizational Systems (or Telling People What to Do 101), and me to Cordon Bleu Cookery.

I know. But Org.Sys. was full when I got around to signing up, and cooking was the only choice left. Fortunately, it was kind of fun. I made a chocolate soufflé last week, and before it fell completely flat, it had a brief shining moment as a thing of beauty. While the chef told us about the project of the day—Eggplant Vindaloo—I tried to get past what Shani had said.

Yes, of course I'd try to find out what was on Gillian's mind, and we'd all help. But did Shani have to bring everything around to boys? Did she have to point out that the "most popular girl in school"—note my finger quotes here—didn't have a boyfriend?

I measured out yellow turmeric, trying to keep it off my uniform because it stains like crazy, while one partner chopped the slender Japanese eggplant into diagonals and the other two worked on the onions and red peppers.

It had taken me months to get over being publicly humiliated and dumped flat by Callum McCloud, who was—thankfully—taking his last term in Europe, like Dani Lavigne. Sure, I liked to look at the guys as they played soccer or pulled the oars in unison, rocketing the Spencer rowing team to a national championship. Again. But looking was all I ever did.

I wondered if the committee would expect me to come up with a big-name date for the Cotillion now that I was senior consultant and the all-too-visible person who would be emceeing the gig. Not that it would change my mind. I had Kaz, and no matter what anyone said, he was going with me. When he put his mind to it, Kaz cleaned up as nicely as anyone—and a lot nicer than some.

Eggplant Vindaloo was an odd choice for a midmorning snack, but hey, we'd made it ourselves, so we ate it. The instructor tasted a helping from a dish presented by each quartet of students and pronounced ours A-worthy. Which was kind of amazing, considering how distracted I'd been.

I was still living in my head when it was time for Phys. Ed. . . . not a safe place to be when the rest of your body is on the volleyball court.

"Ow!" Vanessa spiked the ball straight into my face. If I hadn't ducked at the last millisecond, it would have broken my nose rather than bouncing painfully off my shoulder and into the back row, where Christine Powell dove for it and missed. "Watch it!"

"Pay attention, Mansfield," the ref called. I glared at Vanessa through the net, where we were both playing the front row.

"You heard what she said, Barbie. Or were there too many syllables for you?"

"You didn't have to—"

"Fourteen serving five," the ref called. "Game point."

I already had a bruise on my arm from diving fruitlessly after another of Vanessa's spikes. Clearly, once morning sickness was over for the day, it didn't get in the way of her game—or her bad attitude.

Call me naïve, but part of me thinks that when you do something for someone, that person will thank you for it.

Or at least not call you names for doing it. I didn't expect Vanessa to throw aside her animosity and declare undying friendship in return for a bowl of consommé, but it seemed possible she might at least call a halt to the hostilities.

I cradled my arm in the other hand as we lost the game and trailed into the dressing room.

Evidently not.

chapter 8

ON THE BRIGHT SIDE, the committee meeting that afternoon went well. It took me a little while to convince Ashley and the others that they could have ideas of their own and that every word I said was not martial law. But once I got them deprogrammed, I could see that we were going to work well together and make this the best Cotillion ever.

At four I went back to my room to change and found Gillian already there. But for once, she wasn't surrounded by textbooks, hunched behind her laptop like a warrior in a tower. She lay flat on her back on the bed, still in her uniform. At first I thought she was sleeping, so I tiptoed around, putting my stuff away and opening the fridge door as quietly as possible as I got a bottle of water. But then she sighed and I realized her eyes were open.

"Did I wake you up?" I asked.

"I wasn't asleep."

I don't think I'd seen Gillian lying in one spot doing

absolutely nothing in all the time I'd known her. "Are you okay?"

"I don't know."

"Tell me where it hurts."

I thought she'd laugh, but instead, she fisted one hand and thumped it gently over her heart.

"Aw, Gillian." I sat on her bed next to her feet and rubbed her ankle in sympathy. "What happened? Did you get bad news from home?"

She shook her head. "Nothing like that."

"Then what is it?"

"The same old thing that's been on my heart for weeks."

If Shani was right, there was only one thing that could be. My hand stopped the comforting motions. "Jeremy?"

Her face crumpled and she rolled over to face me, all curled up. "I think I have to break up with him." A tear spilled down her cheek.

"You think you . . ." *Wait. Start again.* "Break up? With Jeremy?"

"He thinks everything is fine. But I . . ." She huffed a shuddering breath. "I don't want to do it."

"Then don't." I hoped I didn't sound as mystified as I felt. "You guys care about each other. You've been together for a year. Why would you want to break up?"

"You don't understand." Her fingers made a pleat in her quilt, over and over.

"I guess not. Tell me."

"He's a great guy. I really like him."

"We all do."

"But he wants more from me than I have to give right now. Oh, not that way," she assured me. It took me a second to realize she was talking about sex. "It's like he wants to make sure I remember him when I'm studying, when I'm rehearsing, when I'm eating. And the more I try to concentrate on what I have to get done, the more he texts me and turns up when I don't expect him. It drives me nuts."

"Have you told him you need some space?"

"He'd think I was giving him the breakup speech." She glanced at me. "I don't know what to do except just . . . give him the speech."

"But you don't really want to."

She shook her head. "I really like him. But I just can't handle it all. My classes, college, my parents, him. It's too much."

"What does Carly say?"

"I haven't told her. The fewer people who know, the better. All I need is for someone to say the wrong thing to Jeremy, thinking they're helping."

Since that was exactly what I'd been thinking of doing, I hastily revised what I'd been going to say. "If this is how you feel, though, he obviously knows something isn't right. It's better to be honest."

"Sometimes honesty can hurt the person dishing it out as much as the person getting it."

"Then you pray about it. And you can be loving, too. It doesn't have to be a verbal amputation or anything like that. Jeremy doesn't deserve it."

"So you think I should do it."

"I think just thinking about it is making you miserable. All of us have noticed. You can't feel any worse than this after it's done, can you?" What did I know? I'd been the dumpee in both my serious relationships, not the dumper.

"I guess not." Gillian sighed. "What are you guys doing tonight?"

I shrugged. "Taking you out for a post-breakup movie?"

"So I can cry through the whole thing? Wow. A good time was had by all."

"There's always dessert down at Ghirardelli Square. We haven't tried Kara's Cupcakes yet. Or the Crown and Crumpet."

She brightened about half a degree. "True. There could be chocolate."

See? This is how it was supposed to work. You show your friend you're concerned about her, you listen, you offer her chocolate. Things become more bearable. And inside, she finds the strength to do what she has to do.

Too bad Vanessa wasn't taking notes.

"Thinking about Vanessa and the way she treats you is a waste of good energy," Carly told me after I'd confided this to her a little later. Shani had gone down to the library to check out some books she needed, so I stretched out on the second bed until she came back.

"I know. You're right. I must be an optimist, huh?"

"I'm glad you took her breakfast, even if she didn't appreciate it. We can only control what we do, not how other people take it." She smiled at me. "Want to come home with me for the weekend? Get your mind off it?"

"I thought Shani was going with you."

"She's starting to panic about her Poli.Sci. midterm. Says she's going to spend the whole weekend in seclusion, studying."

"Hm." I gave this about five seconds' thought. "Gillian and I are going to Ghirardelli Square for cupcakes. How about you guys come with us, and your cousin can pick us up there?"

"We'd have to bring our weekend bags, and our books."

"That's okay with me if it's okay with you."

With a couple of phone calls, we had everything arranged. Then, once we'd all had as much calamari as we could eat in the dining room, we grabbed our bags and headed down to Fisherman's Wharf on the Powell Street cable car.

Once we'd snagged a table at Kara's, it didn't take Gillian long to spill to the others what she'd already told me. Both Shani and Carly looked heartbroken as they realized they were about to lose a charter member of the Happily Unavailable Club.

"I can't believe you'd do that to him." Shani bit into her Raspberry Dazzle. "How can you break up with a guy for liking you too much?"

Gillian's eyes got a little too sparkly, and she blinked several times. "Now you're making me feel selfish. And mean."

Carly swallowed a bite of carrot cupcake before she spoke. "We don't mean to. It's just hard for us to understand, that's all."

"I'd give anything if Danyel would turn up unexpectedly a dozen times a day," Shani said. "This long-distance relationship stuff really blows."

"Maybe there's something wrong with me." Gillian's gaze dropped to her plate, or rather our plate. She and I were each eating half of a Peanut Butter Milk Chocolate Ganache and a nice light coconut cupcake. So far I'd managed to consume both my halves while hers still sat there. "Maybe I just don't have the capacity to care as much as you do."

I blew a raspberry at that notion. "Maybe it's just a simple matter of chemistry. Instead of being Pepsi and Mentos, you're Pepsi and—" I tried to think of an analogy. Chemistry is so not my thing.

"Water?" Gillian gave me a rueful glance and took her first bite. I pushed the plate closer to her and nodded.

"Both perfect on their own, but together, they're just kind of . . ."

"*Meh*," Carly supplied.

"He's not *meh*, though," Gillian protested. "He's really nice and I like him a lot. I need space, and"—she paused and then said in a rush—"and if we're going to colleges in two different parts of the country, what's the point?"

"Have you made up your mind?" I asked her.

She glanced across the table. "Shani and I are both going to have to learn the Harvard fight song."

"Really?" Carly asked. "You decided on Harvard?"

"What program, though?" I knew this was the sticking point for her.

"Pre-med," she said, as though it were the final line of a long argument.

"Not art."

She shook her head. "I don't have to give it up, but what you said the other day stuck with me. I'm going to need some kind of relief valve, and it's not like I can be an art major and take advanced calculus to relax."

"*You* could," Shani pointed out with no irony whatsoever.

Gillian laughed, and then looked surprised at herself.

"That's more like it," I said. "That's the laugh I've been missing since our acceptance letters started rolling in."

"But Jeremy has always known he was going to Davis, and you were going to the East Coast somewhere," Carly said. "Maybe he'll have seen it coming and it won't be so hard. Though if it were me, I'd wait until after the Cotillion."

"She can't hang onto him just to have a date for a dance," I pointed out. "That would make her a user."

"I just don't think I can do it," Gillian said. "Leaving everything else out, he was a good friend to me after I broke up with Lucas and through that whole awful exam-fraud thing. Maybe I'll just have a talk with him. Then, if he decides to break up with me, it will be up to him. At least I'll have tried to explain how I feel."

"And you never know, he might be good with it," I said. "I think it's just a case of him missing you already, before summer even starts. It's like he's storing you up for when he doesn't have you."

"That's so romantic," Carly said with a dreamy smile.

"That's so unlike him," Gillian retorted. "But maybe you're right. I'll talk to him sometime this weekend and just get it behind me. I have to tell him about Harvard, anyway. May as well make it one massive reveal."

"Do you want me to stay?" I asked her. "For afterward?"

With a smile, she shook her head. "No. I'll just hole up in our room and cry. By the time you get back Sunday night, it'll all be over."

Carly's cousin Enrique buzzed her on her phone about then, so in a flurry of paying the bill and grabbing our things, there was no time to talk any further. But on the way down the peninsula in the limo, Carly was so quiet that I could tell she was still thinking about it. When we got to their condo in San Jose, her dad met us at the door and gave us hugs of welcome.

"Make yourself comfortable with us, Lissa," Mr. Aragon said with his warm smile. "I am glad to see you again."

"Thanks for having me. Otherwise I'd be locked out in the corridor while all the other girls bury themselves in exam prep and . . . other stuff."

"And you have no exams to prep?"

"Oh, I do. But my Austen paper is a lot more fun and less stressful than Poli.Sci. or Chemistry. More portable, too. I'll be working on it here."

When it looked like all we planned to do that evening was settle down in our PJs to watch *Enchanted*, Carly's little brother Antony gave up on getting any entertainment out of us and vanished to cozy up to his Xbox. But instead of her normal commentary on costume and character, Carly stayed nearly as quiet as she had on the ride down. Something was definitely up with her, too.

When the movie ended, she shut it off. Everyone else must have gone to bed and forgotten to leave a light on. With the TV off, the room was lit only by the lights of the parking lot outside, across the grassy space between the condos.

I heard her sigh in the dark. "What's on your mind, *chica?*" I asked softly.

Another sigh. "Nothing."

I chuckled. Her profile made a dark silhouette against the other end of the couch. "Nice try."

A second passed, and then she chuckled, too. "I guess, huh." But she didn't go on. Instead, the silence stretched out, punctuated by the wail of a siren in the distance.

"If it were Shani sitting here, would you tell her? Or Mac?" People with boyfriends, who would understand?

Another sigh, and then Carly gave in. "It's my mom."

"Your *mom?*" And here I'd been thinking she had boy trouble, like Gillian. Only, because Carly and Brett really did love each other, it would have been twice as hard to talk about. Not that Gillian didn't care about Jeremy. But Carly and Brett were on a whole different plane of caring. They were the closest I'd ever seen to the real thing. At Spencer, at least.

"She rescheduled her wedding from Christmas to Memorial Day weekend," Carly said.

"Right. You told us that. You also said you might go."

"But *might* doesn't mean I've decided. Lissa, this is killing me. I've beaten the subject to death in my head so much I don't know what the right thing is anymore."

"Have you talked it over with your dad? His feelings are what you care about—what's holding you back."

I felt more than saw her shake her head no.

"Perhaps you should ask him," said a masculine voice from behind us.

Carly jumped about three inches, and collapsed back against the cushions with her hand over her heart. "Papa, you scared me half to death."

The light outlined his hand briefly as he reached over and touched her hair. "I am sorry. I thought you knew I was in my office. Won't you turn on a lamp?" His trousers made a soft sound as he crossed the room and folded himself into the leather recliner by the window.

"Sometimes it's easier to talk in the dark," I said.

"This is true. Especially when the subject is difficult. *Mi'ja*, is it really your concern for my feelings that keeps you from your mother's wedding?"

She hesitated. "Partly."

"I cannot know what yours are, but let me tell you mine. I admit," he said slowly, "that the news of her engagement came as a shock to me. I was not ready to move on, and I could not believe that she could do so that easily."

"Me either," Carly said.

"But people change. What they need from each other changes. Sometimes we can adjust to give them what they need. And sometimes we cannot. I was very focused on giving the three of you a good life, so I worked very hard."

When he paused, Carly put in, "But what we wanted was you."

He sighed. "This I learned too late. But I did learn it. We may live in a small house now, and I may only see you on weekends, but when we are here together, we make the most of it."

"I know, Papa."

"I have learned other things, too. I have learned that the heart can heal if I do not torture it with might-have-beens and what-ifs. If I simply accept what is, then letting her go becomes easier."

Carly sniffled and wiped her cheek with the heel of one hand. Mr. Aragon pulled a white cotton handkerchief from his jacket pocket and passed it to her.

"Please do not hurt yourself any more on my account, *cara*. If you wish to go to the wedding, go for yourself. Do not stay away for me. We do not need any more hurt in this family."

Carly blew her nose. My eyes had adjusted so well to the dim light that I could see her attempt a smile. "I have to say, she needs me. Organization isn't her strength."

"Why? What happened?" I asked softly, hardly daring to break the moment between father and daughter.

"I got an e-mail from her this morning. She finally got the caterer to bring his price down to what they could afford . . . and now the florist is saying the lilies she wanted for her bouquet aren't available."

"Oh, dear."

"These sound like normal wedding difficulties to me," Mr. Aragon said with a smile in his voice. "At our wedding, a flagpole fell over on my car just as we were preparing to leave. We had to begin our honeymoon in a chicken truck borrowed from my uncle."

Carly laughed. "You never told me that."

"I did not want to remind Alicia of our humble beginnings."

"Well, it gets worse. The last thing she said was that she was getting really worried about the wedding dress."

"She's had a dress for months, hasn't she?" I asked. "I mean, she would have had one for last December, right?"

"That one was Richard's mother's. When they postponed, she decided to get one of her own, since they had the time to order it before May. It was supposed to be in the shop in time for fittings, and they keep saying it's coming, but it hasn't shown up yet. There are only two weeks to go before the long weekend."

"It will get there," Mr. Aragon said. "The shop will not stay in business long if its brides do not get their dresses."

"Nothing you can do about it, anyway," I said around a jaw-cracking yawn. "I'm for bed."

Carly got up and hugged her father. "*Gracias*, Papa," she said. "I feel a lot better now."

"Then I do as well. Pleasant dreams, my darling. And you, too, Lissa."

It wasn't until we were settled in bed, with me on an air mattress on the floor, that Carly whispered, "What if the dress doesn't come?"

"Then you whip one together out of a pair of curtains, like Giselle." I yawned again and rolled over, burying my head in the depths of my pillow.

"Hmm," I thought I heard her say before I dropped off into dreams.

chapter 9

ON SATURDAY MORNING, I scoured literary criticism texts while Carly got to work. No, not on homework or midterm prep. On a project much closer to the heart.

Her cell phone sounded like R2-D2 as it autodialed New Mexico. "Mama? It's Carolina."

She held the phone away from her ear while noises came out of it—either raptures or lectures, I couldn't really tell. Not that I was eavesdropping. *Ahem.*

"Mama, slow down. Yes. Yes, I'm coming. I made up my mind last night. Bridesmaid, too, if you still want me. Okay. Yes. I already have a dress, and it's, um, a little more flattering than the poofy one. The bubble look isn't really in anymore."

She rolled her eyes at me and I nodded, pretending to look horrified.

"I know—I got your e-mail. Isn't there anything they can do to hurry it up?" She gasped. "That's terrible. Do you get your deposit back? Well, thank goodness for that. No, listen. Mama! Thank you. Would you like me to make your dress?"

Again she held the phone away from her ear, but this time she was smiling.

"That's why I'm offering. Yes, I mean it. All you have to do is give me your exact measurements—no fudging, Mama, this is no time to be coy about them. Then send me a couple of pictures of styles you like, and I'll design something for you."

Another eyeroll.

"This is what I do, Mama. I've interned with professionals and I'm even teaching. You're just going to have to trust me." Long pause. "I know. But if Papa can move on, so can I, and doing this for you will help me do it. Yes. *Yes*, I mean it, how many times do I have to say so? Send me the stuff today, and whether you want chiffon, satin, or something else, and Lissa and I will go to Britex tomorrow on our way back to school. I'll send you some sketches by Tuesday and pictures of a mockup by Saturday. Okay?"

Another long pause, during which Carly's eyes filled. "I love you, too, Mama. I'm sorry it took me almost a year to say it. 'Bye."

She tipped over onto the couch cushions and blew out a long breath. "Talking with her is so exhausting."

"What happened? The shop's dress really isn't coming?"

"She was nearly hysterical when I first called. She'd just hung up after being told that the factory in Thailand or wherever had closed down, like, two months ago and none of their orders had been filled."

"And they just told her now? Two weekends before she's supposed to wear it?"

"Great, huh? So when I called, she completely bypassed

any guilt trips and went straight to 'You are the best daughter in the world.'" Carly grinned. "Or words to that effect."

"You are," I said simply. "But how are you going to get this done?"

She glanced down at her backpack, leaning against her end of the couch. "I tear through my homework like a tornado and spend the rest of the day drawing designs."

So while I spent the next several hours finishing my paper and slogging through the agony that is a bibliography in strict MLA style, Carly did her homework in record time and then got out her sketchbook. By dinnertime I couldn't stand it anymore and had to go take a look over her shoulder.

Figure after figure moved across the pages, the quick movements of her pencil sketching in clouds of rosettes ("You can buy them already made up") and glimmery trails of pearls ("I really hope she doesn't pick that one, but it was fun to draw"). Trains, halter necklines, fifties peplums, even an Austenlike high waistline ("Your paper gave me the idea").

"That does it," I said, pointing at one particular sketch that took my breath away. "If I ever get married, I'm commissioning you to do that one for me."

"If you ever get married," she retorted, "it'll probably be in a sarong on a beach, and everyone will roast marshmallows for the reception."

"Oh, I'd supply s'mores," I quipped. "But seriously, that one's my favorite."

The female figure looked like a calla lily in a two-piece suit with a tulip hem and a standup collar that made her long neck rise out of it like a bud out of a calyx.

"I like it, too," Carly said. "Maybe I should send it to Kaz so he's prepared. Oh, wait—the groom isn't supposed to see the bride's dress. Silly me."

"Kaz?" I said blankly. "I'm not marrying him. He's my best friend."

"Brett's mine—best male friend, anyway. And I'm not saying never, am I?"

"But you guys are dating. We've never been on a date in our lives."

"You asked him to Cotillion. That's a date."

"I asked him because Danyel is coming and we're all friends and it would be fun."

She gave me a long look. "Do you ever think about how he feels about that?"

My mind flashed back to his odd comments at the time. "He said yes. What's to feel?"

"But would he think you were interested in something else? Something serious?"

Was she kidding? "He knows me better than that."

"You want to know what I think?"

"Do I have a choice?" I grinned at her.

"I think you're using him so you don't have to get out there and be available."

"I'm not ready."

"Callum McCloud was a long time ago. Now that you're Miss A-Lister, you could have your pick."

"Maybe I don't feel like picking. Maybe Kaz is good enough for me. Is that what people are saying?"

"Maybe. I've heard stuff."

And we all knew that Carly's ear for the jungle drums was pretty accurate. "I don't want to do what people expect. I want to be me. And being me means I go to Cotillion with my friends. Have you been talking to Gillian? She was all up in my face about him, too."

Being Carly, she would never dream of saying what was

going on behind those smiling eyes. Instead, she just shook her head.

Totally maddening or what?

TEXT MESSAGE
Kaz Griffin   Phone me quick. Land line—cell out of minutes.
              Mondo urgent!!!

IN MOMENTS I had Kaz on the line. "What is it? What's happened?"

"Are you sitting down?" He sounded muffled, almost out of breath.

"Yes. I'm at Carly's, in her room."

He took a deep breath. "Thomas Nelson bought my graphic novel."

I screamed with delight. He screamed, too—a totally girly scream, but who could blame him? "Kaz, that's fantastic! I can't believe it! After all this time."

"Two years, forty-six days, and twelve hours, to be exact."

"You are totally my hero! When's it coming out?"

"They're thinking 18 months from now. There's some stuff I have to rework, some plot things to change, stuff like that."

"Are you okay with that?"

"Lissa, are you kidding? They publish *Ted Dekker*. I'll do anything they want me to, including sell my soul."

"Don't go that far," I told him, laughing. "It belongs to God."

"I've been waiting for so long I'd almost given up. And

now I feel like I'm flying, like I'm on my board and there's nothing under me but air."

"That's been done already, dude. They call him the Silver Surfer."

He let out a big "Woo-hoo! I'm gonna be published!" and I had to hold the cell phone away from my ear before I went deaf.

"We've got to celebrate," I said. "This is the hugest thing in the history of the world."

"What are you doing next weekend?"

"Coming home to Santa Barbara?"

"Can you bring the Jumping Loon?"

"Uh . . ." I stalled. "She's pretty swamped. Plus she's got, um, personal stuff going on."

"Then I'll come up. I got my license finally, did I tell you?"

"That's two reasons to celebrate. Have you got a car?"

"No, but maybe with the advance money the publisher will pay me, I can finally get that Baja Bug I've had my eye on."

"You can't get a board in a Bug, Bob. Try a truck."

"I hate talking to English majors. Knock off the aLissaration. I'll get with Danyel and see if he wants to come, too. Maybe he'll even let me drive."

"Doubt it. You know how he feels about his truck. Hey, you guys are still planning on coming for Cotillion, right?"

The tiniest pause. If I hadn't already been prepped for weirdness by Carly, I'd have missed it, especially during such an upbeat conversation. "Let's talk about that, okay?"

"What's to talk about? I thought we were set."

"I sold my book!" he shouted instead of replying. What was he—Old Faithful? Blowing off steam at regular intervals? I had to laugh.

"Okay, you get with Danyel and let me know what you guys decide. If you don't come, you should just expect me anyway. This is too good not to share."

"I hear ya. You're the first one I told."

"What, not even your parents?"

"Well, you know Dad. He'll be happy once he sees the check, you know? That's what he considers real, not the pages and panels."

I made a rude noise. "This is real. Didn't I tell you you'd sell it someday? Huh?"

"Yeah, you did. And now I have. Woooooot!"

"Get off the phone and call Danyel, you crazy. And congratulations!"

Laughing, he disconnected, and I looked up to see Carly standing in the bedroom doorway.

"Good news?"

"The best. Kaz sold his graphic novel."

Her eyebrows disappeared up under her bangs as her eyes widened in surprise. "You're kidding."

"Total truth. So they're either coming up here next weekend, or I'm going down there. This calls for a major celebration. I wonder if I can get them to do fireworks over San Francisco Bay."

"You could," she said. "But Kaz probably wants something a little more personal."

"You're right. I have to think of something really special."

She looked at me as if she was going to say something and then shook her head and pushed off the doorframe. "Papa says if you're hungry, we can go over to Santana Row and grab something to eat. He's going to take Antony to see a movie, and you and I can shop."

"That's the second best plan I've heard all day."

I practically bounced as I hurried to change into something to be seen in. Kaz had sold his book! I couldn't wait to give him a great big hug. Surely Carly and Gillian couldn't find anything wrong with that.

By Sunday night I was still feeling pretty bouncy, between finishing my paper and Kaz's news. Even Carly's search for fabric was interesting. Her mother had been lightning fast with responses, as if she thought Carly might change her mind if she didn't do exactly what she said. They'd decided on both design and fabric before we'd left San Jose at three o'clock, and sure enough, she'd chosen the calla lily suit.

At Britex, just before they closed for the day, Carly bought a heavy white *peau de soie* ("It means 'skin of silk' in French—isn't that cool?"), and as we pushed open the front doors of the school and waved good-bye to her cousin Enrique, I could tell she was impatient to hustle it over to the Fashion Design workroom.

"You go ahead," I told her. "I'll take your bag and backpack up to your room."

With a quick hug of thanks, she disappeared down the corridor. I picked up our stuff and as I reached the first landing, I realized there were people on the stairs above me.

"Well, if it isn't the Princess of Whales." Emily's voice sounded way bolder and meaner than I'd ever heard her. "What's the matter, too heavy for the elevator?"

"Bug off," Vanessa snapped. Footsteps slapped the marble, heading toward me, and she came into view on the second-floor landing.

Emily and DeLayne followed her, and Rory Stapleton brought up the rear.

Gross. Boys weren't allowed any further than the stairs

leading to the girls' dorm. And Rory shouldn't even be allowed that far, if you want my opinion.

"What are you staring at?" Vanessa hissed as she passed me.

"Oh, look, it's the new senior consultant," Emily said. "How does it feel to be fired, Vanessa? To know you lost your job because you were fat?"

Hell hath no fury like an overweight Overton scorned. Emily was clearly enjoying the opportunity to turn every insult Vanessa had ever shot at her back on her former BFF.

"Leave her alone, Emily," I said quietly. "It's not right to rub it in."

"I don't need you to defend me!" Vanessa snapped from the landing. "Who asked you, you pathetic poser?"

I turned to give her a piece of my mind. I looked into her face . . . and the light caught the glitter of tears in her eyes. I closed my mouth. These girls had hurt her. She actually cared what they thought. Was that even possible?

Turning back to them, I said, "Emily, DeLayne, come on up to my room. I want to ask your opinion on something the committee came up with."

"Now my opinion matters?" DeLayne's tone dripped acid.

"With all your experience?" I asked. "Of course it does."

"Sure, Lissa." Emily glared at Rory. "Don't you have homework to do?"

"I need to study up on the mating habits of whales," he said with a grin. My hand itched to slap it completely off his face, so it was probably a good thing that he turned and loped down the stairs after Vanessa. I had no doubt she'd take care of the slapping part, if it came to that.

In the meantime, I was stuck with Emily and DeLayne, so in my room, I ran them through the details of the decorations as if their opinion would really make a difference in the committee's plans.

And all the while, I kept seeing Vanessa's eyes. The eyes of a girl who really, really needed a friend.

. . . you do it unto Me.

chapter 10

AFTER I GOT rid of the two of them, I dashed up another floor and knocked on Shani and Carly's door. "Anybody home?"

"Yes," came an unhappy voice. "Come on in." Shani sat pretty much exactly the way we'd left her on Friday, except her clothes had changed. Which, I suppose, was a good sign. "Did you have a good weekend?" she asked, as if she hoped *somebody* might have.

I dropped Carly's bags at the end of her bed. "We sure did. Kaz sold his book!"

She sat back, and some of the life came back into her face. "Wow. That's great. Who to?"

"Ted Dekker's publisher. Can you believe it? He didn't talk money with me, though, so I don't know what the deal was for. We're getting together next weekend to celebrate."

"Here?" She straightened and swung her legs over the side of the bed. "Is Danyel coming?"

"Don't know yet. But Kaz is going to ask him if he wants to. Even if he doesn't, you and I can go down."

She came over and hugged me. "Bless you. You're like a light in a very dark place."

"Wow. Poli.Sci. was that bad?"

"Yep." She looked down at the bags. "Wait a minute. Where's Carly?"

"That's the other piece of news. She and her mom worked it out, and since the bridal shop completely flaked and lost her mom's wedding dress, Carly's going to design and make one for her." I glanced at the calendar hanging on the bulletin board. "In, like, two weeks. We got the fabric this afternoon at Britex, and she's probably in the workroom right now, cutting it out."

"I'm going to go see."

I followed her down the corridor and then waved as she took off toward the Life Sciences wing. This was good. I had other fish to fry. Or stalk, as the case may be.

After twenty minutes of said stalking, I found Vanessa holed up in the back of the library, which is normally deserted on a Sunday night. She looked up from the deep leather chair where she was texting someone furiously, her thumbs practically pushing holes in the keypad.

"*What?*"

Ouch. Every cell in my body wanted to run away, but I took a breath instead and sat in the reading chair opposite her.

She hit Send and held the phone in one hand, as if she expected to answer it.

Or throw it.

"I wanted to see if you were okay," I said.

"No, you didn't. You came to gloat. So do it and get out of here. I'm trying to have a conversation."

"I've got nothing to gloat about."

She rolled her eyes and sighed as if I'd just said the most stupid thing in the world.

"What is with you that you automatically think the worst of people?"

"I'll think what I like. Go. Away."

What was I doing this for? Trying to be a friend to her was like trying to share a cage with an angry tiger. Then I thought of David, who never quite gave up on King Saul, no matter how badly he behaved. "You know, Vanessa, if you weren't so busy being nasty, you'd see I'm trying to be friends."

"You are the last person I would ever be friends with."

"Why?"

"Why?" Incredulous disgust filled her eyes. "Isn't it enough you've taken away my friends, the Cotillion, my lunch table? Why would I want to watch you parade around getting everything you've always wanted? And then you have the nerve to come in here and rub it in my face." She began to pick up her things. "You make me sick."

"That's the baby."

"Don't. Mention. That. To me."

"Why not? It's a fact. It's also the real reason you lost those things, not me. People around here are having a field day with it because they can."

"Like you."

"No." While she had her tote over her arm and she was standing ready to run, she hadn't done it yet. Something was keeping her here. Maybe it was the need to spit vitriol all over me. But on the off chance it might be more than that, I kept going while I could.

"They almost made you cry back there," I said gently. "Those aren't your friends. Why don't you find people who will help you? Give you a smile once in a while, even."

"I'm not interested. There isn't one person in this school who will do anything but diss me. They can all just go to—" She cut herself off and stared down at me. *You are nothing but mold on my shower floor*, those dark eyes said contemptuously.

My shoulders sagged. This was stupid. Why was I sticking my neck out for her when she'd be the first person in line to chop it off? I owed her nothing. In fact, from the way she'd treated me for two years, no one would blame me for jumping on the trash train and dishing out a little of what I'd been getting all this time.

I looked up into her face, getting ready to concede, and saw that her mascara had run just a little and then dried.

She's been crying.

What had I told Carly when we were at her house? *"Sometimes there's a big difference between doing something out of love and doing something because it's the right thing to do."* There was no love lost between me and Vanessa. But I believed in looking to Jesus for my example, didn't I? Sometimes He didn't find love in the people He met, either, but He loved them just the same, and did the right thing. So maybe loving her was stretching it, but I could still do what was right. And then who knew what would happen?

"There might be one," I said quietly.

"Why? What's in it for you?" she demanded.

"Nothing. Except maybe a bunch of abuse. Which I'm getting a little tired of."

"Then leave."

"I thought you were leaving. But you haven't yet. Maybe there's a reason for that."

"Don't get your hopes up, loser."

And with that, she turned on her D&G heel and stalked away down the length of the stacks, toward the door.

Neck, I think you just got chopped.

Then the click of her heels on the hardwood paused. Turned. Came back.

"Ginger ale." The words sounded forced, as though she was pushing them between her teeth against her will.

"Yeah?" I had no idea what she meant.

"On the tray you brought. It helped." She turned and stalked away again, and this time the sound of her heels went right on out the door.

"I think that might have been a thank-you," I told the empty chair across from me in tones of amazement. "Who'd have thought?"

ON MONDAYS AND WEDNESDAYS, Vanessa is in two of my classes: U.S. History and Public Speaking. In the world as I know it, the two of us sit on opposite sides of the classroom, and if we happen to reach the door together, one of us (usually me) finds someone to talk to in the corridor so that no eye contact actually occurs.

But the world as I knew it began to change that Monday. Who knew flat ginger ale could have such a far-reaching effect?

On the way to U.S. History, I greeted people in the corridor and even got on-the-spot updates from one or two Cotillion Committee members—one of whom was wearing a rhinestone love-knot hairband like mine. It wasn't until after her gaze had slid off me and to the side, and she'd waved good-bye and moved on that I realized someone was dogging me.

Vanessa.

As I walked, she stuck by my elbow, close enough so it looked like we might be walking together, yet far enough away that she didn't have to admit to it. And the other students, taken by surprise for the moment, kept their nasty comments to themselves just in case she was indeed with me.

She scuttled into the history classroom and the world was once more as it had always been. But hmm . . . was she using me for protection? I'd told her she needed a friend. Was she taking me up on it? Could I trust her if she was?

"Proceed with caution," Gillian said bluntly at lunch, as I brought the girls up to date on the last couple of days of weirdness. At the table in the window, the sun warmed our backs and we had a prime view of everyone in the dining room—as they did of us.

No wonder Vanessa liked sitting here.

"But what if she's for real?" I sipped my blackberry smoothie.

"I believe God can change a person," Gillian said. "But is that what's happening here?"

"She came this close to thanking me for helping her the other day," I protested. "That's gotta be hard. And it had to mean something."

"That she's not popular anymore and she's reaching for straws to haul herself out of her own hole?" Gillian gazed at me. "I love it that you helped her, and praise God that you did. But it doesn't mean she's going to change. The point is, I care about you. We all do. And we don't want you to get slapped in the face if you try to be friends."

"If you're lucky," Brett said from Carly's other side. "Vanessa's usual weapon of choice is the knife in the back."

"You guys, she was crying," I protested. "After DeLayne and Emily dissed her on the stairs, I saw that her mascara had run. The girl is going to have a hard enough time of it.

Aren't we Christians? Shouldn't we do something to help? Go two miles if a person asks us to go one?"

"Not that Vanessa would ever ask," Brett put in.

"That's just my point," I said. "We're supposed to show the love of God to other people. Her, too. Without being asked."

"Even when they've done something wrong?" Shani wanted to know.

"You can love the sinner, not the sin," Gillian said. "I totally think Lissa is right to pray for her. I've been praying, myself. We can show the love of Jesus that way without standing close enough to get slapped."

Okay, but in the meantime, who was going to walk down the corridor with her or sit with her at lunch? Was I over-thinking this? Worrying about the logistics when I should be thinking about it from a more spiritual standpoint?

"But—"

At that point Shani stepped in and changed the subject, leaving me still wondering what my responsibility was. If I even had any. I mean, I pretty much look to Gillian as my yardstick to measure up to as far as my faith walk goes. She has her struggles like any of us, but she's the first one to suggest prayer while we're problem-solving (not so good for math, but great for life). She's reading her way through the Bible a chapter at a time, and she's got me doing that, too . . . though I have to say, I was really glad to get past the begats and the battles in the Old Testament. So if Gillian says the best thing to do is to pray for someone, you kinda have to pay attention because she's usually right.

But the look in Vanessa's eyes haunted me. The thought of that baby riding around and being taunted and made fun of made me feel sick. I mean, it's been proven that they can hear things in utero, right? How would you like to develop an inferiority complex along with your fingers and toes before you're even born?

In Public Speaking that afternoon, I attempted to take notes during the lecture while the guy who sat at the table in front of us tried unsuccessfully to flirt with Shani. I tuned in abruptly when the instructor said the awful words "group project."

"Many of you are preparing for careers in public life," Mr. Jones said, looking natty as always in a Brooks Brothers suit. "That means you will need to be comfortable in front of a microphone. I want you to separate into groups of three or four and prepare a public presentation based on the material we've covered this term."

I glanced at Shani in alarm. Just how public were we talking here? In front of the class? In front of the school? The city? National TV networks?

"It can be in connection with your community-service activities," Mr. Jones went on, "or in aid of a school event. It can even be performance art. But it can't be part of any drama or theater performance you're already doing, and you must be filmed or recorded in some kind of public capacity that has been rehearsed beforehand. I'll hand out a sheet of prompts and ideas, and in the meantime, you can divide into your groups and brainstorm."

Shani grabbed my arm before he'd even finished speaking. "We are so a group, girlfriend," she said. "I have no idea what to do, but I'm not going in with Tate DeLeon and his buddies or the math geeks."

Mr. Jones came around with the sheets and handed one to each of us. "How many in your group?"

"Two."

"I said three to four, Miss Hanna."

"We're good." She gave him her best marketing smile. "The two of us can do the work of four, trust me."

"I'm sure you can, but that's not the nature of the project." He looked around, counting off the numbers in the groups that had already formed.

"Not Rory," I whispered. "There will be homicide, I swear."

"Miss Talbot, are you in a group?"

"No, sir. I've had a lot of public-speaking experience at the school, as you know. I'd like to waive this project, please."

"I'm sure you would, but I want total class participation. This is a life skill and you wouldn't be enrolled here if you didn't feel it was useful to your future. Therefore, you'll join Miss Mansfield and Miss Hanna. Stapleton, you too."

I stifled a scream just in time.

"I'm already in a group, Mr. Jones."

The instructor looked him over, then at Tate and two other jocks from the rowing team. "I'll expect great things from this group, Stapleton."

Rory just grinned at him, but Shani and I practically wilted with relief. Being in contact with Rory Stapleton for any reason whatsoever would totally spoil the last month of senior year.

"Miss Talbot, please join the others at their table. For the last fifteen minutes of the period, do some brainstorming and let me know what your project will be as you leave."

Vanessa acted as though she were wading through peanut butter as she moved to our table. She dropped her backpack on the floor, draped herself in a chair, and examined her manicure.

"Yeah, well, we're not a hundred percent happy about it, either," Shani said in a low tone. "So. What's our project?"

Vanessa slid the sheet of project prompts off the table and into her backpack. Then she gazed at the clock over the door.

Tick tock.

"Oh, I get it. We're going to do all the work, and you're going to take the credit," Shani said brightly. "Well, that's buckets of fun. Let's get started. Lissa, any ideas?"

"The only public thing I've got going this term is the Cotillion," I said. Vanessa's left shoulder twitched, but she made no other indication she'd heard us. "I'll be emceeing, introducing guests, introducing the non-academic awards, and all that. So how can we all get involved?"

"Divide it up."

"Okay, if the—"

"Absolutely not," Vanessa snapped. "That's the point of the senior consultant. She manages the planning, so her reward is visibility on the night."

"Oh, are you part of this group?" Shani inquired. "I thought you just sat there because the view of the clock was better."

"I'm trying to help you idiots not fail."

"Can you suggest something, then?" I asked. "Personally, I don't care about being visible. But if we have to do this project, unless you're prepared to do some performance art at the cable car terminus at Powell Street, it makes sense to use an event we're already involved in."

"*We?*" Shani inquired silkily.

"It's *we* now," I said.

Heaven help us.

Uh . . . wait a second. What if this was Heaven's plan to bring Vanessa closer to us? College might not be high on God's priority list, but what if she was?

chapter 11

A S WE LEFT the class, I told Mr. Jones our group would be working on the Cotillion. Vanessa once again slipstreamed me as I made my way down the corridor.

"We should talk," she said when I'd looked back and caught her eye for the second time. "Do you have to walk so fast?"

"I have Art now, and it's all the way at the end of the building." The art studios were above the music practice rooms, which was kind of neat. I could always tell when Gillian was at the piano on the floor below—it made me feel as though I were making jewelry in the middle of a symphony.

"What about after school? We could walk down and get a latte. Throw some ideas around."

"Sounds great. I'll let Shani know."

"I didn't mean her."

My stride hitched, and she came up beside me. A couple of people looked at us oddly (*Why is the most popular girl in school walking with that skank?*) but no one said anything. "Why not?"

"She's a b—"

"Okay, enough of that. No one calls my friends names in front of me."

In one of those odd instances of perfect timing, two girls from Phys.Ed. made a big show of crossing to the other side of the corridor when they saw Vanessa. They hissed a nasty word at her and giggled as if it was the funniest thing in the world.

She kept her gaze straight ahead. "Guess I'm not your friend, huh?" I had no idea what class she was going to—or if she bothered to go to some classes at all—but she kept pace with me.

"Do you want to be?"

I couldn't tell, since she wore her usual this-conversation-is-boring-me-into-a-coma face. All the same, if this really was part of a bigger plan, I needed to listen to that voice inside that never steered me wrong.

Blessed are the peacemakers, for they will be called the sons of God. Or daughters, as the case may be. Decision made.

"Okay," I said. "I'll meet you at Starbucks at four. That'll give us an hour before dinner." She scrunched up her mouth as if I'd offered her a plate of worms. "Say what you want, but I like the food here."

With a nod, she cut away down the corridor toward the science labs, leaving me wondering what I was getting into.

So, ninety minutes later, I pushed open the door at Starbucks to find a smattering of Spencer blue cardigans at the various tables. Vanessa sat in the back next to a rubber plant, looking very studious with an enormous biology textbook.

Maybe she was studying up on what exactly happened

during labor—a section I knew was in there, even though I hadn't been assigned to read it during my brief and not-so-illustrious career in science.

I got a skinny vanilla latte and joined her. She slid her backpack off the leather chair next to her and I sat. "So. The Cotillion."

Whoa. Clearly the girl didn't believe in small talk.

"I was thinking we'd just divide the programming up among the three of us," I began as she put the Bio book away. "Instead of me doing the whole job all night, we'd each take a section. And it's being videotaped, so that meets Jones's requirement."

"It'll never fly," she said flatly.

"Why not?"

She looked at me as if my brains were dribbling out my ears. "Hello? The only reason you have this job at all is because . . . ?"

Because the committee didn't want you up on that stage. Right. "But if your getting involved again is a requirement for a class, nobody can say anything."

"Uh-huh. They might not say anything, but you'll find that, hey, it's the last week before Cotillion and all your teams suddenly have homework to do or they're on field trips or they have seventy-five hours of community service to catch up on."

"My team won't do that."

"Are you willing to take the risk?"

I thought of the phenomenal amount of work ahead of us. We'd hired lighting crews and a band and caterers and an event planner, but the success of the dance still depended on the smooth operation of my various subcommittees. People had to interface the band with the sound system, and the caterers with Dining Services, and the lighting riggers with Facilities. If even one of them flaked, the whole operation would tilt dangerously into panic mode.

"Shani can take part of the emcee job," Vanessa said quietly. The scope of what she was suggesting must have shown on my face. "But if you expect to include me, you might have to change your project."

"None of us has time to come up with anything else," I said. "This is tailor made for us. We just have to think creatively, that's all. Or, hey, just not tell anyone you're part of it, and hand you the microphone at the last minute."

"*You* think creatively. I have to go."

"Wait a minute." I grabbed her arm and out of sheer shock, she plopped into her chair again. "You can't say let's get together and discuss this and then not discuss it."

"I just did."

"Telling me it's impossible isn't a discussion."

"I don't hear you coming up with ideas."

"Hello, I've had five whole minutes to think about it."

"And look what that got you. People would find out if you planned to bring me in at the last minute. Your friend would flap her mouth for sure."

"Maybe. Though maybe if you were nicer to her, she wouldn't."

"She isn't nice to me."

"It has to start somewhere."

"Don't preach at me, Christian girl."

Something snapped in my brain and unraveled like a rubber band wound too tight. "You know what you need, Vanessa? You need a good spanking. You say you're trying to help us succeed, but you're not. You're just using us for whipping girls to take out your rage on."

Silence fell over the entire coffee bar, as though a cloaking device had just been activated.

My voice felt rough in my throat as I dropped the volume. "News flash, girlfriend. You got yourself pregnant, and people are taking advantage of that to get you back for years of snottiness and abuse. But not all of us are. Some of us feel sorry for you. Some of us would support you if you'd let us. But no. All we get is more of the same. Are you really that one-dimensional, or is there a real person in there who is going to make this baby a decent mother?"

Vanessa stared at me, her mouth open a little and her eyes positively burning a death ray through me. "Are you quite finished?"

"No. I'm not." The noise level around us rose a little. "Yes, I'm a Christian. But what that means is that I can feel. I can empathize. I can try to be your friend, but you're too busy calling me names and dissing my friends to see that."

"I don't want your empathy. Or your pity."

"Maybe not. But what you do need is a friend."

"Why should you care?"

Because God is love, and compassion, and all those things you need right now. And I may not be much, but I'm the closest thing you've got to Him, sister.

"Maybe I'm just that kind of person. But you've never given me a chance to be who I am."

The corners of her mouth twitched. "There's more to Surfing Barbie than meets the eye. Who knew?"

"Maybe. And maybe there's more to the PeeGee Princess, too."

Her gaze held mine for a couple of seconds. "That still doesn't solve the Cotillion problem."

"Maybe not. But I'd like to think it solved a few others."

Her lips twitched again. Then she chuckled. And finally she threw her head back and laughed—a real laugh. I had never seen Vanessa Talbot laugh before, ever. Sneer derisively, sure. Snarl, bait, smile, and tease, yup. But never laugh.

Neither had anyone else in the coffee bar. People gawked, and some sophomore actually whipped out her camera phone and took a picture.

It was contagious, too. When she finally got control of herself, both of us were smiling. "All right, Barbie," she said at last and shook her hair back. "You've got more spine than I gave you credit for."

"Truce?" I said, just to be sure.

"Truce. We have work to do."

"Friends?" I pressed. As Mac would say, in for a penny, in for a pound.

"I wouldn't go that far." But her lips twitched again as she said it.

The Ginger Ale Effect? Or the power of God?

I had a feeling they were the same thing.

. . . .

✉

To: caragon@spenceracad.edu
From: strathcairn3@scotmail.co.uk
Date: May 17, 2010
Re: Gossip

Hey, lassie! (How do you say that in Spanish?) I miss you too— thanks for the pic of your mum's muslin. That's what you call it, right? The practice dress. I hope she realizes how amazingly talented you are, because that is going to be one beautiful wedding ensemble.

I got a note from Shani and I'm still quite in shock. Lissa and La Talbot friends? I'd be less surprised if you'd told me Posh and Becks had grown out their hair and joined a commune. How is this even possible? Vanessa hates Lissa. And our L is too trusting for her own good. I'm very much afraid it's all a ruse and V is setting her up for some horrific fall.

Watch out for her, will you? I told Shani the same. Lissa's heart is in the right place but sometimes her head is . . . blond. Don't let her get hurt.

Dad sends his regards, and Mummy says please come for a month before you start college. She's going to be mucking out the attics and wants an informed opinion on some of that old clobber. Namely: museum, jumble sale, or PREZZIE FOR YOU. Hee hee. I'm not too proud to resort to bribery.

Please come!!

Love, Mac

....

PRAYER CIRCLE IS the one place where a person's true feelings can come out—where you can feel safe letting them out.

And no one showed her feelings more than Carly, who sat opposite me, practically glowing. Why? Because sitting next to her was Brett, who, she had texted us all, had asked her what he needed to do to become a Christian. Yes. Brett Loyola, scion of one of San Francisco's wealthiest families, captain of the rowing team, former bad boy . . . giving his heart to God. Can we just pause for a moment to appreciate that?

I know they've talked about faith stuff in private. The whole "no sex before marriage" discussion came up right away last spring, when they first got together, just in case he had other ideas. But there's a difference between talking about something and acting on it, as I had been proving myself this last week or so.

I was dying to ask her if he was going to church with her on Sunday, but it would have to wait until later. As it was, I exchanged a sparkly glance with Gillian that was as close as we could get to "Squeee!" without saying a word.

There was a lot of praising going on in that room, so when my turn came around, I just let it rip.

"Father in heaven, I am really glad to be here tonight to see all the unique ways You show love to Your children. Your face is really shining on Carly, with her mom and Brett and Parsons and FIDM and everything. Thank You for that. So tonight I just really want to praise You for getting me past Vanessa Talbot's deflector shields and helping us connect. Help me be the friend she needs, Lord, and help me be as transparent as glass so she can see You without me getting in the way. In Jesus' name, amen."

There were a couple of ticks of silence before Derrik Vaughan, who was sitting next to me, began to pray, and when I glanced at Gillian again, her eyes were closed and her face had become solemn. So, okay, I hadn't really talked to her since yesterday. She and Jeremy—still officially together as far as I knew—had decided to take Monday night off to let their cortexes unkink and had gone to a movie, and I'd been asleep when she came in. Consequently this morning had been a rush of nearly sleeping through the alarm and throwing clothes on and rushing down to breakfast. So I hadn't had a chance to tell her about the breakthrough in Starbucks.

I looked forward to telling her the details. I mean, prayer is a good foundation for a change in any relationship, but then you have to act, right? So both our philosophies could be right in the long term.

Big picture or deets, I didn't get a chance to say any of it. After we finished up with a contemporary praise song, the whole group seemed buoyed along by happy spirits and wound up at the juice bar down the hill.

So much for BFF dishing time.

Or so I thought, until Shani climbed onto the high stool next to me with her ginger and lemongrass in a tall, slender glass. "So." She flipped out her phone and tapped her way to a familiar-looking photograph of a laughing Vanessa, the back of my head on one side of the frame. "What's the story here? Word is you and the PeeGee VeeTee had a big public blowout."

"I heard you threatened to spank her." Carly put her handbag on a stool to save the latter for Brett, who was still at the counter, and got comfortable across from me.

Shani snorted juice and clapped a napkin to her face. "You just made me spew!"

"I told her that was what she needed. I didn't volunteer to do it."

"Did I really hear that?" Gillian paused in the act of pulling up a stool. "*Spanked?*"

Brett and Derrik Vaughan joined us, both carrying glasses of something revolting and green.

"What *is* that?"

"Wheatgrass and carrot juice." Brett took a big swallow. "All the guys on crew drink it."

"Ewwww," we chorused. I knocked back half my organic unpasteurized apple juice in sheer defense.

Brett waited until I was finished. "So it's true? You and Vanessa decided to forgive and forget?"

"I think she needs a friend," I said slowly. The juice tasted like a bite of a fresh-picked apple, like late summer when I was a kid and the only complication life held was the big red circle on the calendar that meant the first day of school. "Mr. Jones put her in a project group with Shani and me, so we have to work together. But I think it's something bigger. A God thing."

"Maybe it is. This is not the face of someone forced to work together." Shani waggled the phone at the group before she put it back in her bag. "I can't believe you guys met without me."

"She insisted. She says you're not nice to her."

Shani's eyes bugged out. "Me? Not nice to *her*?"

"I told her it went both ways, and she told me not to preach. That's when I lost it and told her she needed a spanking. But it ended well, so that's the main thing."

Brett chuckled into his glass. "I'd have bought a ticket to see that."

"I would, too," Gillian said. "We might have to start lifting up *Lissa* in prayer circle at this rate."

"Speaking of prayer circle, what's all this about Parsons and FIDM?" Brett nudged Carly with his shoulder. "You holding out on me?"

Carly shot me an agonized glance.

Uh-oh. Prayer circle was good for a lot of things, but clearly there was such a thing as too much truth. Especially when you appeared to be keeping it from your boyfriend.

chapter 12

"PARSONS?" DERRIK REPEATED. "Is that in SoCal? I've never heard of it."

"It's a design school in New York City," Gillian told him. "Carly, did you get accepted there?"

She nodded, then looked at Brett. "But don't worry. I'm not going."

His shoulders relaxed. "That's good. You can't go that far away. Berkeley's a great school. You'll like it."

"Um, actually, I'm not going there, either."

Brett's hand jerked so that the remaining juice in his jumbo glass sloshed halfway up the sides. "What?"

"Can we not talk about this here?"

"Why not? I mean, when were you planning to tell me? Where are you going?" Then his face cleared. "Oh, I get it. You got accepted at Stanford, too. That's even better!"

She pulled away from his hug. "No. I picked a school that's not even in the Bay Area."

From where I sat, all the way across the table, I could see the color drain out of his face. "What?"

"I'm going to the Fashion Institute of Design and Merchandising in Los Angeles," Carly said quietly. "They only accept a few people every year, so it was a huge deal to get in." She held his gaze with hers, her expression soft. "Be happy for me. It's my dream come true."

"Your dream? What about us? What about that dream?"

"Um, guys?" Jeremy looked as uncomfortable as I felt. "Maybe you should talk about this in private."

"Too late now," Shani muttered. "What goes on in prayer circle isn't staying in prayer circle."

"I want to know now," Brett said. "Los Angeles? Why?"

"If I'm going to have a career as a costume designer, I need to be close to the movie industry," Carly said. Her eyes had begun to glitter, probably from distress at having to have this conversation in front of all of us. "And FIDM is the tightest thing there is as far as costuming and design on this coast. I'll still be in California." Her voice took on a pleading tone. "We can see each other at breaks and long weekends."

"But that's not what we planned."

"We?" she asked. "You knew I applied at schools away from here."

"Yes, but I didn't think you'd walk away from me for a bunch of clothes." Brett stood up. "I gotta go."

"Brett, wait. No one's walking away." Except him.

He held up both hands as if to ward her off. "I can't deal with this right now. You talk it over with your friends. They know more than I do about everything in your life, anyway."

"I'll come with you, man." Derrik got up and the two of them pushed their way through the tables and out the door.

"Brett!"

Shani grabbed Carly by the arm as she started to run after

him. "Give the guy some space, girl," she said. "You can text him later when he's calmed down."

"But—"

"Listen to her," Jeremy said. "Brett's got a temper on him. Let him get past it or you'll just make things worse."

Carly's lips trembled as she grabbed her bag. Her face was white as she looked at me. "Did you *have* to say that in prayer circle?"

"I didn't know you hadn't talked about it with him," I wailed. "It was a happy thing. It just came out."

"It's not a happy thing now." She shoved her bag under her arm and walked to the door.

"I'll go keep her company and make sure she doesn't run after him." Shani picked up her two-seasons-old Prada clutch and followed her.

Gillian gazed at me from one end of our now-empty table. Another customer swiped Brett's chair and pulled it over to where a new group was forming. "It's not your fault," she said.

"I feel like it is." A lump formed in my throat and my voice wobbled. "Prayers are supposed to be good things. They're not supposed to *hurt* people."

"They are good things," Jeremy told me. His nice brown eyes were so sympathetic. "How could you know they hadn't talked about it?" He put an arm around Gillian's shoulders. "I'm glad that's one discussion we've already had."

"What, colleges?"

Gillian's dark eyes skewered me, as if to stop any more words from coming out of my mouth.

Jeremy nodded, looking as happy and innocent as if . . .

. . . as if Gillian hadn't given him the breakup speech. Yet.

Well, I wouldn't be taking *that* down to Room 216 and praying about it. I learn from my mistakes. I make a lot of them, but I do learn.

Eventually.

<hr>

✉

To:	lmansfield@spenceracad.edu, vtalbot@spenceracad.edu
From:	shanna@spenceracad.edu
Date:	May 19, 2010
Re:	PS idea

I've got an idea for how we can get V in on this Public Speaking project. Meet me on the slope behind the music rooms after school.

How are your community service credits looking? This will solve that, too. I tell you, I'm brilliant!

Shani

<hr>

NOTHING EXCEPT DETENTION would have kept me away from the meeting place after school. Since Art is my last class of the day on Mondays and Wednesdays, I didn't have far to go—just down the stairs at the end of the corridor and out the door.

Shani arrived a few minutes later, and Vanessa arrived fifteen minutes after that. Like we expected anything less than complete consideration for our valuable time. Not.

"So, what's so brilliant?" she asked, folding herself onto the lawn next to me.

"Oh, we already had the meeting. See you." Shani pretended to get up.

For a second, Vanessa actually fell for it. Then she seemed to realize this was Shani's way of letting her know she didn't appreciate the late arrival. I sighed and braced myself for a snarkfest.

Vanessa settled back. "Sorry I was late. I popped my head in to ask Dr. Vallejo something. We got talking and I lost track of time."

Something pregnancy-related? Neither of us had the nerve to ask.

To her credit, Shani merely nodded and matched her practical tone. "No problem. So, here's my idea. What if we turned the video of the Cotillion into a short feature?"

"Like, a movie?" I asked.

"More like a documentary. In fact, I was thinking that if you started right away filming the preparations for it—like a couple of committee meetings, and the run-up stuff to the actual event, Vanessa could act as the narrator. Then the classes that come after us would have a how-to guide for putting a Cotillion together."

"They wouldn't have to reinvent the wheel every year," Vanessa said. "What a great idea."

Shani looked surprised. I bet she'd expected to get shot down in derision and flames. I know I had.

"You really are brilliant," I told her. "The stuff that happens right before the night is really important—you know, our teams working with the companies we've hired. If we filmed it, it would be exciting and a huge information resource as well. I mean, not everyone knows how to get ahold of lighting guys and riggers." I hadn't worked as a production assistant for my dad for nothing.

"How do the community service credits come in?" Vanessa asked. "Not that I need them. I wrapped mine up in junior year."

Of course she did.

"You'll have to decide whether you want to do this or not, Lissa," Shani said, "but what if we made the Cotillion a charity event as well? Say, add ten bucks to the ticket price and donate the money to the Share Literacy program or a summer camp for creative kids?"

"And the video could incorporate that," Vanessa said. "I could do the segment on the charity and how the money will be used. I've worked with Share Literacy before. With a phone call I could get it all set up."

Literacy program? Underprivileged kids? Vanessa?

It took me a second or two to line up this new dimension with the person I thought I knew. But then, what did I know about how she spent her free time? Sure, some of it was partying and shopping, but obviously a portion of it had been spent tutoring kids in reading. Now there was a visual for you. Vanessa Talbot sitting on the floor with a kid, pronouncing letters and taking time to listen to halting words. Wow.

"Perfect," I said at last. "Let's do it. We only have a month to go, so there's no time to lose. Who's going to hit up the Media and Communications teacher?"

"Um, hello? Ashley?" Vanessa said.

"Huh?"

"Use your team, Lissa. Ashley Polk practically lives in the Media/Comm lab. Only you'll have to leave me out of it or she'll never agree to add this to what her film crew is already doing on the night."

"We can film your segments ourselves and do the voice-overs later," Shani said. "I mean, how hard can it be? Mac puts little movies together on her computer all the time."

I prevented myself from commenting on that one. It had been one of Mac's "little movies" that had gotten Shani into horrendous trouble involving angry royalty and black helicopters last Christmas.

"Settled," I said. "I'll ask Ashley, and Shani, can you run this by Mr. Jones and make sure he agrees that Vanessa's doing this for the school is the same as public speaking in front of live people?"

"Got it." She climbed to her feet and grabbed her messenger bag. "I bet he's still there. I'll go ask him now."

"Thanks, Shani," I called after her. "You really are brilliant."

"I know." She laughed and vanished around the corner of the building.

"I'm meeting with the committee on Friday," I told Vanessa, gathering up my tote. "I'll run the charity angle past them and get Ashley's buy-in then."

"Do you have to go right away?" she asked.

I stalled. "Uh . . ."

"Or do you just not want to be seen with me in public?"

"Of course not. What are you talking about?"

"People could decide they don't want to be friends with you anymore if they see us out here talking."

"Then I'd be left with the friends I started with, which are the only ones that matter to me," I retorted. "I don't care if people see us talking. What, do they think pregnancy is contagious?"

"People's opinions are," she said. "I'm just giving you the option."

"If popularity depends on who I'm seen talking to, I don't need it."

Her laugh held the mocking note I was used to. Not as much, but it was still there. "You are the most politically inept person I've ever met."

"Thank you. I'll take that as a compliment. What did you want to talk about?"

"Oh, I don't know." She stretched her bare legs in their Santana sandals down the gentle slope and leaned back on her hands. The pose exposed the growing bulge of her belly, which was putting severe strain on the seams of her plaid uniform skirt. It was almost like she was making a statement: I'm not afraid to show you the truth about myself. Because it was a fact that everywhere else—in the corridors, in the dining room, in class—she wore her cardie or her school blazer to cover up as much as possible.

"Okay, then, maybe you can tell me something."

She glanced at me, her dark eyes made up with a faultless hand. "What?"

"What are you going to do when the baby comes?"

For a split second I expected her to (a) get up and leave, (b) throw something at me, or (c) spit in my eye. But she didn't. The look in those eyes changed, though, to something more penetrating and dangerous.

"How is that any of your business?"

"It's not. I'm asking as a friend."

"A friend." She looked away. "A friend who will blab it far and wide, with pictures at eleven."

"No. I might be convinced to offer a little moral support, though."

"Moral." She snorted. "Right. I so need that."

"Bit late now," I quipped.

She paused, and then to my surprise, she laughed. "True. Well, to answer your nosy question, I have so many options I can't pick one, thanks to our helpful school administration."

"What do you mean?"

"They assigned me a private counselor practically the minute I missed my period. I'm supposed to talk to her once a week, and if I miss the appointment, Ms. Curzon is on the phone five minutes later. At the moment I'm doing what I'm told by Dr. Vallejo. She's freaking. Keeps telling me she's not an obstetrician and I should be under the care of someone at Stanford. Then she hands me lists of vegetables and vitamins."

"You mean you haven't been to a proper baby doctor yet?"

"No."

"But how else will you know what to do?"

She shrugged. "Why bother when I may just get an abortion?"

My jaw sagged and hung open. Was she saying this to shock me, or did she really mean it?

"Don't look like that. There's still time."

"You wouldn't."

"Why not?"

"Because it's wrong, that's why." On so many levels. "And what do you mean, there's still time? Nobody would do the procedure when you're so far along."

"You'd be surprised who will do what, given enough incentive."

My stomach rolled and I wondered if I was about to throw up.

"Good grief, Lissa—chill. It's not that big a deal."

"Having an abortion is a huge deal. I can't even say how huge it is. Please don't do it. Please."

"It's my decision."

"I know, and you must be having a hard time making it or you would have done it three months ago."

Her lips, wearing pale pink lipstick, thinned to a grim line. "Mind your own business."

"Hey, you wanted to talk."

"Talk. Not be told what to do."

"Someone has to tell you. If Dr. Vallejo and your counselor aren't all over you about it, then . . . what about your family? What do they say?"

She stared at me. "What do they have to do with it?"

"Or the baby's father's family. Do they even know?"

"No, of course not."

"You didn't tell the dad?" I asked in amazement.

She scrambled to her feet. "How dare you talk to me like you know anything about it! I thought you'd be understanding, but you're just Christian Barbie, all plastic and fake. Push your button and you preach."

"Vanessa!" Tears prickled in my throat. How could she think that? "Help me understand. Why won't you let anyone help you?"

"Like you're helping me? Dishing out accusations and making me feel even worse than I already do?" Her cheeks had flushed red and furious tears glittered in her eyes.

That made two of us.

"I'm sorry. Please. I hate that I made you feel that way when I didn't mean to. But . . ." I gestured at her belly. "That's a baby in there. I don't understand how you can talk about flushing him out like a hairball in the drain. He's a *person*. He deserves to be taken care of."

"Great," she snapped. "You can adopt him, then."

I might have been shaking, but I didn't back down. We faced each other across a verdant few feet of lawn. "That's a better option than the flushing. I'm not accusing you, honest. I'm just telling you the truth. It would be wrong to do what you're thinking. Please don't kill the little guy. Give him his chance."

I couldn't believe we were even having a discussion about killing anything. I couldn't even kill a spider—if I found one in our second-floor room, I carried it to the window and encouraged it to go outside.

Vanessa dragged in breath after breath as if she'd been running. Then her jaw dropped and all the expression fell from her face. Her eyes gazed into the distance—or into the future, I couldn't tell. She covered her belly with both hands.

"Hey. Are you okay?"

"He moved," she said in a faraway voice. "Just now. He's swimming. I can feel him."

"Sit down." I pulled her down next to me. "You're all right? No water breaking or anything?"

She slid me a glance and pursed up her mouth. "We have a few months to go before that happens, you goof."

Whew. *That* was normal, at least. What a relief.

Her hands still lay on her belly. "He stopped. Wow. That was weird."

"Is that the first time you've felt him?"

"I woke up a couple of nights ago from a dream about giant goldfish. Maybe that was him."

"It could be a her."

She shook her head. "It'll be a boy. I know it."

I took comfort from the fact that for the last few seconds, she'd been using the future tense. Like maybe the little guy was going to have one.

chapter 13

I TRACKED DOWN ASHLEY Polk after dinner, before I got started on my horrid chemistry homework. She texted me that she was out at the playing field, so I jogged over there to find her in the bleachers, watching the boys' soccer practice.

I filled her in on the revised plan for the Cotillion.

"Good thing we haven't sent the tickets to the printer yet," she said, writing notes on her ever-present PDA with a slender stylus. "Summer Liang can change the price and add a line about the charity. And what a great idea about the video! If I'm elected senior consultant next year, that'll be the first thing I show the new team of juniors."

"If I weren't graduating, you'd have my vote," I told her with complete sincerity. "You're so good at this." I thought she blushed, but the setting sun was behind her and I couldn't tell for sure. "If you ever want to intern with a charity organizer, I can put in a word with my mom."

"Thanks, Lissa, that's really nice of you," she mumbled,

slipping the PDA back into her bag. She jumped to her feet to cheer a spectacular save by the goalie, then settled down again.

"Friend of yours?" I inquired. He looked familiar. I blinked my contacts into place.

"Derrik Vaughan." She sighed. "I wish."

Of course it was Derrik. I'd just never paid that much attention to the boys' soccer team before. "He seems nice," I said. "He came with us for coffee last night after prayer circle."

"Prayer circle?"

I nodded. "Every Tuesday night at seven in Room 216. He's come the last few times. You'd be welcome, too, if you felt like it."

"Oh, no." The words sounded like a groan, and she actually moved a couple of inches farther down the bench. "I thought it was just a rumor."

"What? That he's coming to prayer circle?" Wow. The rumor mill must be over Vanessa and hurting for new material.

"No. That he's going there for you."

I stared at her. "You lost me."

"Word is he's going to ask you to Cotillion."

"That's silly," I said firmly. "First of all, he's never said more than hello and good night to me, and second of all, I already have a date to Cotillion."

"You do?" Like a parched flower that has just gotten a shower of life-giving rain, Ashley straightened and the brightness came back into her face. "You don't like Derrik?"

"Of course I like him, the way I like everyone in prayer circle. But I don't *like* like him. I like—" I stopped. *I like Kaz.*

Well, of course I did. He was my best friend. But did you have to like someone as a boyfriend to go to Cotillion with him? Of course not. That would complicate things way too much.

But all the same, I'd better shoot him a note to confirm who was going in which direction this weekend to celebrate his book deal. And maybe we'd find some time for a little talk. I needed to prepare him for what people would think if he came as my date. I mean, he'd pretty much saved my skin last year at the Benefactors' Day Ball, turning up at the last minute so I wasn't left standing partnerless and pathetic in the spotlight. So it probably wouldn't surprise anyone to see me on his arm this time. But it might surprise *him* if people made assumptions about us that weren't true. I didn't want him to be embarrassed.

And if a girl wanted to dance with a nice-looking guy like Derrik who seemed to appreciate her, well, it would be better if that was ironed out beforehand, too. I mean, technically I was a free agent.

Not that I'd ever steal Derrik if Ashley were interested in him. We'd worked together enough that I'd come to like her as a friend. Her support on the Committee was half the reason I was able to lead it. And, let's face it, my Public Speaking grade depended on her cooperation. Three very good reasons not to poach. But there was nothing wrong with a dance with him, was there? Or being friends? If there was one thing I was good at—besides shopping and organizing stuff—it was making friends.

Ashley and I parted ways, with her looking cheery and promising to do everything she could to help with our video project. Guess I should have let her know I had a date to Cotillion ages ago. In any case, I was feeling pretty cheery myself by the time I got back to our room to face horrid chemistry.

Gillian looked up as I came in. "Hey."

"Hey, stranger. I hope you're in a coaching mood, because I'm going to need it." I got my chemistry books out and thumped them on the desk, then fished out my Air. Through the open window, I heard someone down on the lawn give a high-pitched giggle, and the smack of a ball against a guy's hands. Clearly they were not in my chemistry class.

"Sure," Gillian said. "Thirdterm prep, huh?"

"Yes. And Milsom hates me, so that always makes it worse."

"You'd think five months of marriage would have mellowed him out."

"Marriage to Ms. Tobin?" I gave her an are-you-kidding face and we both laughed.

For two hours I suffered through the prep sheets of questions Milsom had handed out that morning, and by nine thirty could take no more. "I'll finish the rest in free period tomorrow," I groaned. "Must seek chocolate. Do we have anything in the fridge?"

"I ate it all while I was doing my Mandarin essay translation. Sorry." Her apologetic expression told me all I needed to know about how difficult *that* had been.

"Back in a minute." I grabbed my change purse and headed down to the vending machines that lived under the staircase. Once I had a Snickers bar in hand, though, I decided that with thirdterms coming up next week, I'd better stockpile some more. In between the sounds of quarters dropping in the slot and candy bars thunking into the tray, I heard murmured voices out on the staircase.

"Go on. Now's your chance," a guy's voice said.

"I can't," somebody else whispered.

"The chick is never alone. It's now or never."

By the time I'd straightened, hands full of chocolate in all its blessed incarnations, Derrik Vaughan stood in the doorway of the little room, his face beet red. "Hi."

Ashley's happy face flashed in my mind's eye. "Hey, Derrik." I held up my treasure. "I'm recovering from chemistry burnout. I hope you weren't looking for Snickers bars, 'cuz I just cleaned them out. Unless you want to work out a deal."

"No, I, um . . . I was looking for you."

I smiled at him. Poor guy—he looked so uncomfortable. Even though he was six two in his stocking feet and could call the captain of the rowing team one of his best buds, he was kind of cute when he blushed. "Here I am." When he didn't say anything, I filled in the silence. "Was Brett okay? Last night after prayer circle? I still feel kind of bad that I opened my big mouth about Carly's plans."

"Yeah." Then alarm flared in his eyes. "I mean, not yeah, you have a big mouth. Yeah, he's okay. At least, he didn't mention anything about it after that."

Of course not. He was a guy. Did guys ever talk?

"He and Carly will work it out," I said with confidence. "See you later." I angled past him in the cubbyhole doorway.

"Um, Lissa?"

"Yes?" Now both of us were wedged into the cramped space. He needed to back up or go forward. "Why don't you—"

"I was wondering—"

My armful of chocolate bars began to slip, like a fan opening.

"Are you going to Cotillion with anyone?"

"I—no, ack, help!" The bars tipped out of my hands and began to slap on the linoleum, one, two, three. We both bent to pick them up at the same time . . . my butt hit the door-frame by accident . . . I bounced off it, straight into his arms with my hands full of rescued candy.

My foot landed on his and I lost my balance, staggering against his chest. "Oof!" His arms closed around me and I pulled back to apologize. I mean, could there be a bigger klutz in the entire school?

I heard a telltale click as somebody's camera phone went off in our faces, freeze-framing us for posterity locked in each other's arms, gazing open-mouthed into each other's eyes.

I was so dead. Ashley Polk was going to murder me.

By the time I'd gathered up the landslide of chocolate bars and gotten myself upstairs, a fit of the giggles had set in. Poor Derrik had vanished at top speed, not that I could blame him.

I let myself into the room and dumped the candy onto the end of my bed.

"It's about time." Gillian, in her pajamas, sat cross-legged checking e-mail. "Did you have to go all the way down Fill-more to find a shop that was open?"

The giggles burst into a real laugh as I told her what had happened. "I doubt poor Derrik will be asking me to Cotil-lion again. . . . After all, if I can create a disaster in a four-by-six space, just imagine what I could do in a ballroom."

Gillian's full-throated laugh was music to my ears. I'd missed that sound. "You know, Jeremy said something about Derrik and you, but I was rehearsing and he was talking and I didn't pay attention. So he really asked you? What did you say? Before the chocolate bars escaped captivity, I mean."

"I didn't get a chance to say anything. It would be lame to send him a text saying no, huh?"

"Um, yeah."

"I guess I'd better track him down tomorrow and apologize for being such a gumball. Hey, speaking of Jeremy, I take it you haven't had The Conversation with him yet?"

The smile faded from her face. "No. I have to do it, though, before he asks me to Cotillion."

"You mean he hasn't yet?"

"Why would he? I mean, if I didn't have this hanging over my head, I'd assume we were going together. It would be natural, right?"

I nodded. "But what are you going to do if you give him the talk and he asks someone else?"

"That's a risk I'll have to take. Is it selfish to hope he doesn't? I want to go like you and Kaz are going. As good friends. Though I've gotta say, it sure takes some of the sparkle out of it."

"Why should it? It's going to be a very sparkly party."

A wistful look seeped into her eyes. "What's a dance without romance? I'd have to skip all the slow songs, unless I wanted big gobs of awkward."

That had never occurred to me. But then, neither had I ever slow-danced with Kaz. Ballroom stuff, sure. But romance is the last thing on your mind when someone is counting out the beat in your ear and saying things like, "Get off, Liss. I need that foot."

Gillian eyed me. "Are you sure Kaz isn't expecting a little romance with his dance?"

"Of course not. You guys need to stop thinking that way."

"You are so weird. Kaz is hot. I just don't get why you can't see it."

"Hot?" Wow, she hadn't even given Jeremy the speech and

clearly the mourning period was already over. "Of course I know he's hot. And he has a nice smile, which is even better."

"And eyes that adore you, and all that thick wavy hair to run your fingers through."

"Gillian!"

"Well, he does. And he's tall and toned and—"

"If you want him, *you* should take him to the dance. Sounds like you've got enough romance on your mind for both of you."

"Temper, temper." She was enjoying this, the rat. She held a hand to her ear. "Is that barking? Do I hear a dog in the manger?"

"Shut up."

"We don't want him for ourselves, but we don't want anyone else to have him, no, my precious-s-s-s."

"It's not like that at all!" I protested.

Then what was up with this tight, angry feeling in my chest? And the sudden urge to growl at her for even thinking about Kaz's surf-toned self? Huh?

No, no. I couldn't be this way. If I got all jealous and possessive now, just talking about it, what would happen if Kaz danced with someone else the way I had thought of dancing with Derrik? What if I made Ashley feel like this? How crummy would it be to do that to a girl I considered a friend?

Grrr. Argh.

I pulled my phone out of my tote.

TEXT MESSAGE

| Lissa Mansfield | Hey. What's the plan for this weekend? |
| Kaz Griffin | Just talked to Danyel. He's on board. And he'll let me drive his truck on I-5. |

Lissa Mansfield	I'll notify the CHP.
Kaz Griffin	Funny girl. We're staying at his sister's.
Lissa Mansfield	See you first thing Saturday? I'll get with the girls and come up with plans.
Kaz Griffin	Sounds good. See ya.
Lissa Mansfield	xo

As soon as I hit Send on that last text, I wished I hadn't signed off that way. Would he take it wrong? Then again, I signed off on e-mail that way all the time. He might think I was mad at him if I didn't include a hug. Should I have just done the "o" and not the "x"?

Should I stop overthinking now?

I'd better get my feelings together before the weekend. Kaz was no dummy. If my emotions were bouncing all over the place, he'd see it and want to know what was going on. We'd always been honest with each other, and clearly I needed to talk things out with him.

Just as soon as I figured them out myself.

"Kaz and Danyel will be here Friday night," I reported. Gillian had brushed her teeth and climbed into bed while I was texting. "We need to plan something fun."

"Then you'd better plan for Shani and Danyel to disappear. They haven't seen each other since spring break."

True enough. "Okay. Nothing that requires tickets bought in advance. Or a car, since they'll probably use his truck."

"We can rent a car. Even if Carly and Brett come with us, the Camaro can only take two extra."

"Three if you sit on the hump in the backseat."

"If anyone sits next to Kaz, it'll be you."

"Why not you? You were all hot for him a minute ago."

"I wasn't hot. I was just pointing out the positive."

"Hmph. Can we not talk about this?"

She snickered. "Sure. Let's talk about your second favorite subject. Vanessa Talbot. Please tell me the rumors aren't true."

With a sigh, I took the bait. "What would those be?"

"That you're giving her Christian counseling so your mom and dad can adopt the baby."

An incredulous hoot of laughter shot out of me. "You've got to be kidding."

"That was the *nicest* rumor. I'm not passing on the other ones. You should be careful, Lissa. I really hate hearing stuff like this about you. It hurts."

My heart softened. "I've only had, like, three conversations with her. She's going back and forth about getting an abortion. If I can convince her not to, then all this talk will have been worth it."

"I'm glad you're talking to her about that. But where's Dr. Vallejo in all this?"

"Dr. Vallejo talks about vegetables. Vanessa needs a friend. And at the moment she seems to be listening to me."

"Have you ever asked yourself why?"

"Uh . . . because I'm the only one in the school who's speaking to her?"

"I just think you should dial it back a bit, that's all. I mean, what does she want? A friend to talk to? Or to latch onto your popularity and hope it spills onto her? How can anybody really know what that girl wants—or what she'll do to get it?"

I stared at her. Since when did Gillian care about popularity? Wasn't she the one who was always telling me that people's opinions didn't matter, that it was who you were in God's eyes that counted?

"Who are you and what have you done with Gillian Chang?"

chapter 14

I SHOULD HAVE KNOWN things could only go downhill from there.

"Okay, so that was shallow," Gillian said. "But, seriously, I'm only thinking of you. Hanging with Vanessa isn't good for anyone—look at Emily and DeLayne. I've heard they were fairly normal before they got sucked into Vanessa's group. DeLayne and Shani actually used to be friends when they were freshmen. I just don't want to see you turn into a clone like they did, that's all."

"If you think that would happen, you don't know me very well," I said. "And there's more to it than this Public Speaking project we're doing together . . . or the baby."

"The project I understand, but I'd really like to know about the baby," Gillian said. "What do you mean, there's more to it?"

"I don't know. This pregnancy thing makes her seem more human." I amended that. "She *is* more human. I've seen her mocked and hissed at in the hallways, and I know at least twice it's made her cry. I mean, yeah, she's been horrible to me since the day I started here, but I'm trying to do the right thing. Not dish nastiness back, you know? After all, didn't Jesus say we aren't supposed to give someone a stone if they ask us for a fish?"

"Vanessa isn't asking."

"I think she is. She just doesn't know how to do it without losing face. Anyway, she hasn't even seen a proper doctor yet. I don't know why. She's got a private counselor; you'd think they'd be on her constantly about it."

Gillian slid under her brightly embroidered quilt and pulled it up to her chin. "Okay, I get that she needs a friend. But I still think you should protect yourself in case she decides friends are overrated and she doesn't need you anymore. I mean, 'Come out from among them and be ye separate,' not to mention 'Touch not the unclean thing,' are in the Bible for a reason."

"That was talking about Egyptians and food, not doing things for people out of the goodness of your heart."

"Was not." Gillian sat up and took her Bible down from the shelf above her pillow. "That's from Second Corinthians, and Paul was talking about the people of God hanging out with unbelievers. See?" She showed me the chapter and verse.

"Oh." Still. "Being kind to her will go a lot further than just pretending she doesn't exist. Which would be hard, now that we're doing this project together."

"I'm not saying don't be kind to her. We all should do that. But my problem is with watching you go further and trying to be friends. I know it's going to backfire and hurt you, and that's what upsets me. You heard what Brett said. Vanessa isn't capable of being a friend. She doesn't do things out of the goodness of her heart. All she can do is look out for Number One, no matter who she climbs over in the process."

"She reads to underprivileged kids, Gillian. That has to say something."

"For community service credit. You might stick up for her now, but you know the first time push came to shove, there you'd be, out in front of the speeding bullet with her handprints on your back. I just don't see how you can forget that she posted your make-out session with Callum on the school server for everyone to laugh at."

"I'm trying to forget it. But it's not easy when you keep bringing it up."

"Can you honestly say you've forgiven her for doing that?"

Okay, that wasn't fair. "We never proved it was her."

"Of course not. She's too smart to get caught. But we all know she set you up to use her room, and then accidentally on purpose left that webcam running."

"So now you don't want me to forgive? You want me to disobey what Jesus said?"

"Of course not," she said impatiently. "Forgive her. Pray for her. I certainly do. Just don't hang out with her and let yourself in for whatever her end game is."

"Doesn't that make you a hypocrite?" She stared at me. "You pray for a person and forgive them, but you won't be friends with them?"

"I pray for Rory Stapleton, but I certainly wouldn't want to be in the same room with him," she retorted. "That's not hypocrisy. That's just understanding him and being smart."

"Oh," I said in a bright tone. "Now I'm not smart. Not like you, the smartest person in this school now that Lucas Hayes, your *other* ex-boyfriend, is gone." Her face smoothed out and set into that expressionless look she gets when she's hurt.

My stomach went hollow as I realized what I'd done. But still my mouth kept talking, spilling stuff out while my brain screamed, *Stop!* "It's nice to know how you really feel about me. Maybe I don't have as much in the brains department as you do. Maybe if you'd tried for the Hearst Medal, you'd have come in first, not second. Fine. But don't quote the Bible at me when all you want to do is sit around and judge someone. Meanwhile, I'll be off trying to show the fruit of the Spirit to somebody who's never been exposed to it before."

I stomped into the bathroom and slammed the door closed between us.

"I'm not judging her," Gillian shouted. "I'm trying to protect you from her. Why are you mad at me for caring about you?"

But I turned on the water in the shower as hard as it would go and drowned her out.

TEXT MESSAGE ————————————————————

Carly Aragon	Where RU?
Lissa Mansfield	In the bleachers, doing homework and watching soccer.
Carly Aragon	?? Be right there.

CARLY CLIMBED UP the bleachers and sat next to me in the top row. Out on the field, the center forward from Sacred Heart, the city's defending champion, made a breakaway and blasted toward Derrik in the Spencer goal mouth. Our defense closed in to stop him, but he twisted like a greyhound and drilled the ball over Derrik's left shoulder. The home crowd groaned while Sacred Heart clapped their center on the back and jogged back toward the line.

"What's the score?" Carly asked.

"Six to three. We're losing."

"Isn't Derrik Vaughan our goalie?" She craned her head to see, but Derrik, his head down and his hands on his hips, was talking to the ref with his back to us. Carly gave me an *aha* look. "Is that why you're out here? To watch him?"

"No. I'm out here because I can't stand being inside right now. In fact, if I had a car, I'd be heading straight west to the beach with my board."

"And you can't stand being inside because . . ."

I sighed. "Gillian and I are still fighting."

With a sympathetic nod, she said, "I know. She told me."

Great. "And what did she say?"

"Just that it's about Vanessa. She doesn't think you should get any closer to her."

"Is that what you think?"

"I don't know what to think. I want to be as loving as I can to everyone. Even Vanessa. But it's hard when she's never made any effort to be nice to anyone else."

"Carly, if Jesus had that attitude, none of us would ever have the chance to know God."

"We can only do the best we know how with what He told us. And He said to be good to those who hate you."

"That's what I'm trying to do. Ergo, Gillian is mad at me when she's the last person who should be."

"I don't think it's about that. It's not about popularity or what people think or anything. She's just trying to protect you."

"That's what she said, but I don't need protecting. I'm not a little kid. I need support."

Carly fell silent for a few minutes, watching the game pick itself up and go on. Then she straightened and shook her hair back. "Come on," she said. "You're not concentrating anyway. I've got something to show you."

I slid my U.S. History books into my tote and let myself be led into the Life Sciences department. Truth? I hated fighting with Gillian. Hated, hated, hated it. It spoiled everything, and made it so that even eating in the dining room became fraught with politics and maneuvering and emotional fallout.

But how could I back down and tell her, okay, I'll lose Vanessa and you and I will go back to being friends in our safe little lives, where we all have each other and nobody makes mistakes and gets huge responsibilities dumped on them when they're not prepared?

I couldn't bring myself to do that when I'd come so far with Vanessa. The baby had moved and she'd shared that with me. It had to mean something, right?

Carly opened the workroom door and I realized with a start why she'd brought me here. "Don't tell me you've finished the dress for your mom already."

On the other side of the room where the mannequins were, one stood off by itself. I recognized the design immediately.

"Not the dress. But the muslin is done."

"Wow," I breathed. I dropped my tote on the floor and circled the mannequin slowly. She'd made the muslin out of plain cotton broadcloth, but even so, the skirt's lines were smooth over the dress form's hips and the jacket collar furled away from the back of its neck just as it had in her drawing. "How did you get it to do that?" I touched the neckline.

"After careful consultation with Tori Wu and about a dozen tries, I finally figured it out. It's all in the interfacing and a teensy bit of boning. Now I have to take it all apart and cut the *peau de soie* from the pieces."

"How do you remember where everything goes?"

She shrugged. So modest. So Carly. "It's all in my head. The skirt is a simple sheath, and the sleeves are plain, except for the petal wrap at the wrist. Most of the wow factor is in how the collar will frame her face." She ran her finger down the line of it. "I just have to convince her to wear her hair up. Otherwise no one will be able to see it."

"She'd be crazy not to. And not too much veil, either—maybe just two lilies on one side of a French twist." I turned to her. "So you and your mom are okay? No guilt? No needling and pointed reminders?"

"Not one." Her face softened. "Once my dad showed me that it was okay to move on, everything seemed to change. I even phoned her the other night and apologized for ruining her Christmas Eve wedding. She was so sweet. She said that it would be much better this way, starting off her new marriage with forgiveness and hope instead of with resentment and regret."

"Wow. That's different. From what you've said about her, I mean," I said hastily. I'd never met the woman, only heard her on the phone.

"I guess I've been kind of unfair to Richard," she admitted. "I mean, I still think his fashion sense needs to be locked in a room with Tim Gunn for a week, but his heart is what counts when he's marrying my mom. She seems different with him. More . . . settled."

Carly smiled as she picked up my tote and handed it to me. I waited in the corridor while she tidied up the work-room and closed it. "I'll start cutting tomorrow."

"Wait. What about Kaz and Danyel? They'll be here first thing."

"Oh, I'll be happy to see them—we could do breakfast together. But I need to get this done. The wedding is next weekend and I have to fly out on Thursday night to do the final fitting Friday."

"What about Brett? Does he want to come?"

She looked away. "I don't know. You should ask him."

"Carly." I touched her hand. "You guys aren't still fighting, too, are you?"

"We're not fighting." But she wouldn't look me in the eye. "We're giving each other some space to come to terms with the future."

"Have you been reading psych textbooks again? What does that mean?"

Her shoulders sagged. "It means we're still fighting." She sounded miserable, as all the light and pleasure that her mom's dress had brought drained away.

Darn relationships anyway. "Join the club."

"I haven't done anything wrong. If I had, I'd have apolo-gized. So that makes it hard."

"I hear you. Hey." I stopped. "Want to go for supper at The Cheesecake Factory?"

"The one in the top of Macy's?"

"Is there any other?"

"I don't have any money."

"I have a Platinum Visa, and I know how to use it."

"Deal. Meet you out front at five."

Relationships were painful, and wonderful, and a constant

struggle to figure out how to do the right thing. But spinach dip and caramel cheesecake could make everything better. At least for a while.

I couldn't seem to make Gillian happy, but at least I could do something, no matter how trivial, for Carly. And right now, that was good enough for me.

chapter 15

BAM-BAM-BAM!

"They're here!" Shani hollered through the door. "Danyel just called from the guest lot."

"Coming!" I called, giving my hair a last once-over with the brush and doing a quick check of my outfit at the same time. I loved the floaty, flimsy Marc Jacobs babydoll top with a contrasting yellow tank underneath, all over white capris and Liberty Print Nikes.

Knowing I was styling a great look that Kaz would probably like partly made up for the fact that Gillian was nowhere to be found. I soon learned the reason for that as Shani, Carly, and I dashed across the lawn toward the guest parking lot overlooking the playing field.

She'd beaten us to the boys.

With a shriek, Shani flung herself at Danyel, who whirled her around in a bear hug. Carly hugged Kaz, his six-foot self bending to wrap his arms around her.

Gillian had already gotten her dibs in, it seemed, because she stood behind him, grinning. Hmph. I swear, if that girl was making a play for Kaz, I was going to—

"Lissa!"

I threw my arms around him and hugged him hard—which meant I noticed three things simultaneously. One, he'd filled out some more since I'd been home at spring break. Either that or there'd been some serious workout action going on. Two, he smelled really good—*Pour Monsieur*, if I wasn't mistaken. Since when did Kaz worry about cologne? Was that for Gillian's benefit? And three, I was enjoying this hug way too much.

Back away from the man, girlfriend.

Regardless of what these girls thought, I knew Kaz. And he didn't think of me like that. It would be way too embarrassing if I got all heated up over him. If he found out, he'd probably run into the sunset screaming, or he'd laugh at me, which would be ten times worse. And then things would get all weird between us, and I'd lose my friend.

I wouldn't let that happen. I'd keep my moment to myself and not let it spoil things.

"Congratulations on the book deal!"

"Thanks." He released me and stepped back. "Today is all about the celebration, so prepare yourself."

"Hey, Lissa." Danyel hugged me with one arm, the other still around Shani.

"You really let this guy drive your truck, with his head up in the clouds?" I asked him, elbowing Kaz in the ribs. "Are you nuts?"

"Only on the freeway. Once we got to the city, I wasn't taking any chances."

"Clouds or not, I wouldn't drive on these hills, especially with a stick shift," Gillian chimed in. "Sometimes I get vertigo just walking up them."

"Have you guys had breakfast?" Carly asked. "The dining room's open, but only until ten."

"If they're staying with Malika, they probably already had a nice tree-bark stew with unshelled nuts on top." Shani gave Danyel a big faux smile.

"At least she can cook," he quipped, which netted him a punch on the arm. "Yeah, we ate already. And it wasn't tree bark. It was bacon and eggs."

"So we're off to the beach, then?" I said, all hopeful eyes, even though there didn't seem to be a board of any description in the back of the truck.

"Lissa's idea of fun is to give you more of what you already have at home," Gillian said.

"That's not—"

"I have a standing invitation at Brett's vineyard in Napa," Shani interrupted. "Mrs. Loyola said we could spend the day up there, even if Brett's got a regatta today."

"Um, awkward." I nudged her and glanced at Carly, who was looking in the direction of the Life Sciences wing with longing.

"Oh, I'm not going with you." Carly turned back to us with guilty haste. "I'm working on my mom's wedding dress today. The five of you should still go. Six, if Jeremy's in."

"Napa's more fun with you and Brett along," Danyel told her. "Next time. I'm good with just kicking it down at the waterfront, if you all are game. That way we can hoist a crustacean in Kaz's honor."

I'd glanced at Gillian at the mention of Jeremy's name, but that smiling face didn't give away a thing. "Where is Jeremy?" I asked brightly. "He wouldn't want to miss that."

"Don't be so sure." Gillian's tone was completely normal, but she didn't meet my eyes. "He said he was studying."

"So we have the chicks to ourselves," Kaz said with satisfaction, looping an arm around Gillian and me. "My kind of odds. Bring on the cable cars."

You will not fume. Gillian's the third wheel, not you.

I tried to tell myself that as we collected our handbags and caught the train to Powell Street. Even as we swooped down the hill toward Chinatown, Kaz and Danyel whooping and hollering on the outside rails of the cable car as though they were on a roller-coaster ride, I laughed and joked as if this new attitude of hers totally didn't bother me.

Why, then, did I tense up every time Kaz called a comment to her, or she teased him about something? I didn't do that when she razzed Danyel. Nope, I needed to talk with Kaz, stat, before Gillian got any more fun ideas in her head.

I got my chance after the promised crustacean toast to Kaz's success in the publishing business. We'd just dumped our empty shells and sourdough crusts in a trash can when Shani and Gillian got distracted by something in a shop window, further down the strip opposite Fishermen's Wharf. I seized the opportunity, not to mention Kaz's arm, and walked him around a corner in the other direction, toward Ghirardelli Square.

"Wait, we'll lose them." He looked back over his shoulder.

"We all have phones," I reminded him. "I haven't had a second to talk to you since you got here. They'll understand." We walked up the hill, silent, while I tried to figure out where to start. *So, what's going on between you and Gillian?* seemed too blunt—and on the off chance that nothing was, I'd just look weird.

I sighed. Talking with Kaz wasn't usually this . . . fraught.

"You okay?" He was nothing if not perceptive. "It's a shame about Jeremy, huh?"

"Yeah. Who wants to study instead of doing something fun?"

"No, I mean about him and Gillian breaking up."

I stopped dead in the middle of the sidewalk. "What?"

"Sometime this week. It's too bad. I thought he was nuts about her."

"Wait. Whoa. Gillian and Jeremy broke up and I'm just hearing about it *now*?" My chest hurt, as if I'd been stabbed. "Who told you?"

"One guess, Sherlock. Gillian's not in the habit of saying things that aren't true. You seriously didn't know?"

"We . . . well, we haven't been getting along too well lately. A difference of opinion about something. But that's no excuse for not telling me. I mean, she hasn't cried about it or anyth—" I stopped. Nor had she allowed herself to be around where I'd see it. She could have cried her eyes out in the girls' bathroom and I wouldn't have known.

Shame washed over me. It takes two to fight, and I'd nurtured my hurt and defensive feelings as if they were a prized African violet. Because of that, my best friend had to suffer on her own. What was the matter with me? Here I thought I was pretty good at discernment, when I couldn't even detect a breakup in my own roommate's life.

"Liss, you're not going to cry, are you?" Kaz bent to look into my face. "Because all I've got for you to honk on is my T-shirt and I like this one."

I gave a watery chuckle and blinked the tears back. "That's okay." I peered at his chest. "The *Abbey Road* album cover is safe from me."

He straightened, relieved, and we walked on. "So, what are you two fighting about?"

"I didn't know you were that close to her." I needed time to work up an answer he'd understand, so I opted for a conversational swerve. "A breakup isn't the kind of thing I'd tell a guy friend of my roommate."

"Oh, we e-mail all the time." We climbed the steps into Ghirardelli Square and by mutual accord headed in the direction of the chocolate shop. It had a big window where you could see the candy machines stirring fudge and vats of chocolate. "At first it was just about graphic art, and then we got to be friends. I'd help her out on a project; she'd help me out on physics. Ugh."

"That'll teach you for not taking it last year."

"Right, Miss Chemistry-Is-Killing-Me."

Touché. "If it weren't for Gillian, neither of us would have made it through midterms."

"So she asked me one time about guys, and then I'd talk to her over e-mail, you know, about stuff."

Stuff. That could cover a multitude of things. "What stuff?"

"Boy-girl stuff."

"You could have talked about that kind of thing with me." The knife in my chest turned, just enough to hurt again. "You and I talk about everything. After all, who got me through the whole Callum debacle? And Aidan before that?"

"Your taste in men is questionable."

"What does that say about you?" I shot back.

"I'm not going out with you."

"You're going to Cotillion with me. That's, like, a date." *What's a dance without the romance?* Gillian's wistful voice echoed in my memory. I shook it away.

"Is that what you want it to be?"

I searched his tone for a hint of the way he wanted me to answer, but there was nothing. It was just a question. One with about fifty different answers. I settled for the safe one. "I don't know."

Eyes front, he sighed and gazed through the window at the lady rolling out a big sheet of fudge. "You sure take a lot for granted, Lissa. I never actually said I'd go with you."

Fear stabbed me. "You don't have plans that weekend, do you? You have to come. It will be fun."

"That's all it is to you? Fun?"

Where was he going with this? What kind of answers was he fishing for? "Sure. Dances are always fun. And a bunch of work, in this case. I have to emcee the whole thing, so I'll be running around with a Bluetooth on my head instead of a nice sparkly hairband."

"So if I didn't come, you wouldn't really miss me. You'll be busy producing."

"Not true. We'll all sit together and dance together. All our friends at the same table." He turned away from the window. "Don't you want to buy any fudge?"

Shaking his head, he said, "Nah. I'm not in the mood for sweets."

That was a first. What was the matter with him? Was it something I said? Was it the wrong thing? What did he want me to say? Talking with Kaz had always been effortless and transparent, like water running in a comfortable creek bed. But now I felt like I was bushwhacking my way through an impenetrable jungle with a pair of nail scissors.

"So," he said in a changing-the-subject-now voice, "you were going to tell me what this difference of opinion is between you and Jumping Loon."

"What, besides the fact that she thinks you're hot?"

That surprised a laugh out of him. "She does?"

"Don't get a swelled head over it."

"It's nice to know someone does."

"Why would you say that?"

"You just said she thinks I'm hot. And you said that wasn't the only difference of opinion you had with her. Ergo, you don't think I'm hot."

"If I did, I certainly wouldn't tell you." I tried to make it sound like I was teasing, but it fell flat. "You seem to be a little low on humility this morning." Oh, dear. That sounded like criticism, which was the last thing I wanted.

"Unlike some people, who can't make up a fight with their friends because . . ." He waited for me to fill in the obvious blank.

"That's not the same thing."

"Tell me."

I latched on to the change of subject with relief. I'd much rather talk about Vanessa than about whether I thought he was drool-worthy. Which I totally did, especially after this morning. Never let it be said that my friends could spot a cute guy before I did. But this was Kaz. Our relationship operated on a higher level. Sure, he was tall and buff and could control a surfboard on a twenty-foot swell as if he were born in the waves. And he had dark brown eyes with long lashes, and half a dozen freckles that drove him crazy, and cut cheekbones and a great mouth and . . .

"Lissa?"

I blushed as if he could read my mind and see the treacherous path it was taking. "You remember Vanessa Talbot?"

"Dark hair. Killer clothes. Toxic, back-stabbing harpy."

"Right. Well, she got herself pregnant over Christmas while she was in Italy."

"Whoa. And this has what to do with anything?"

"We've sort of become friends."

He gawked at me in amazement. "The one who posted the video of you making out with McCloud? The one who sent the Yasiri Secret Service after Shani when you guys were in Scotland? The head of the A-list? We're talking about that Vanessa?"

"She isn't the head of the A-list now." I told him everything—the breakfast tray, why I was suddenly senior consultant, the mockery in the halls . . . all leading up to why Gillian and I had come to the edge of a disagreement that yawned like a great big chasm between us. "So that's where I'm stuck," I concluded unhappily. "And why my first best friend had to tell me about my second best friend's breakup. I honestly didn't know."

"Wow," Kaz breathed. "Five minutes to process."

We wandered through Ghirardelli Square and out the other side to the waterfront. I checked my phone to make sure it was on. No messages. The other three were either (a) being incredibly considerate, (b) had no idea we were missing, or (c) two of them had ditched the other, who didn't want to send up a flare for us and admit it.

We sat on the grass near the seawall and watched the sun dance on San Francisco Bay. Alcatraz rode a thin cushion of mist out in the middle, and the Bay Bridge linked the two sides together, busy with lines of traffic heading back and forth from Oakland. The scent of salt water and dried kelp blew toward us on the breeze, and from under Fisherman's Wharf away on our right, a couple of sea lions barked at each other, *orp-orp-orp*.

"Here's how I see it," Kaz said at last.

Oh, good. This was what I needed: my friend, with whom I'd talked everything out since grade school.

"First of all, you're both sisters in Christ. You've got to make things right with Gillian before anything else."

"I will," I promised fervently. "I can't stand it that she's hurting and I made it worse."

"Second of all, you can pray about it together, then pray for Vanessa together."

"But there has to be more than prayer. It's wrong to leave someone to the wolves if it's in your power to help."

"Sure, it is," he said with quiet patience. "But Gillian obviously thinks Vanessa can handle the wolves. It's you she wants to keep out of their way. You can show her your way works and let that speak for itself. No more fighting about it."

"I'm glad you think being kind and being a friend will work." My emotions had been up and down like a cable-car ride this morning. I was feeling touchy and raw.

"I think it's part of who you are to try, Lissa. Whether it works is up to God and Vanessa. But I wouldn't want you to stop trying."

Abruptly, tears threatened again. "So you support me? Even if Gillian thinks you're hot?" Oh no, *that* wasn't what I'd meant to say.

He slung an arm around my shoulders and squeezed. "You know I support you in spirit. It's just that sometimes . . ." His voice trailed off.

"What?"

He glanced at me. "I don't think I can come to that Cotillion gig with you. Not the way things stand."

My mouth opened and hung there, empty of words. That wasn't just a swerve. That was a hairpin turn with a dizzying drop off a cliff.

"I'd come if you wanted me there for *me*. Not if it's just convenient to have a friend to call so you don't have to mess with the social scene at Spencer and challenge Vanessa again. No." He held up a hand, cutting off my protest. "It wasn't Gillian who said that. I may be just a guy, but I can figure some stuff out on my own."

"That's not why! I asked you because you're my best friend."

"Maybe that's why I can't come." He stood and waved, and when I finally thought to move and look in that direction, the others had joined him.

Weren't we all just having a wonderful time?

chapter 16

NEEDED TO DO one thing before this day got any older. I went up to Gillian, pulled her away from the others, and gave her a big hug.

"I'm so sorry I've been such a *mo guai nuer* all week. Please forgive me."

Her body, which had been stiff with tension and resistance, wilted and she hugged me back. "Me, too. I've been horrible to you all day. I feel like garbage, but that's no excuse."

"Kaz told me. Why didn't you say something?" She pulled back, and in her eyes I saw the answer. "Never mind. How could you talk to a snowbank?" I asked rhetorically. "When did it happen?"

"Yesterday after lunch. I felt awful. His face . . ." Her own crumpled at the memory, and I fished in my bag for a tissue. "Thanks."

"But he understood, didn't he? Are you guys still friends? Or is that too much to hope for?"

"I don't know. On all counts."

"But he'd pick up if you called him, right?" That was always a good indication that there was hope.

"I haven't had the guts to try. It doesn't matter, anyway. I left my phone in the dorm."

I hugged her again, and we turned back to the others. "You guys okay?" Kaz eyed us both with honest concern. It was enough to make a person want to hug him, too.

"Yes," Gillian told him.

"I'm sorry about Jeremy." Shani gave her a hug. "Kaz just told us. That totally blows, but you had your reasons."

Gillian nodded. "You guys, this weekend isn't about me and my lousy timing. It's about Kaz and his book. Can we not talk about it and just have fun?"

The vote was unanimous. "Who's for renting a sailboat and taking it out on the Bay?" Kaz asked.

"Only if you steer," Danyel told him. "I wasn't born in deck shoes like some people."

The rest of the afternoon was a breezy blur of sails and sunshine and laughter. I remembered enough from last year's sailing class to help Kaz with the sheets and canvas, and every time he hollered "Jibe!" I made sure everyone's heads were down by the time the boom swung over to change our direction.

Sailing is just enough work to keep you alert and active while leaving your brain free to think. And I needed to think, now that Gillian and I were okay. I needed to figure out what part about being my date to Cotillion had bugged Kaz so badly that he didn't want to come.

Was I going to have to pin him down and ask him to tell me point-blank what he was thinking? Because clearly I wasn't very good at reading the signs. Did he want to take our friendship to another level—to boldly go where neither of us had been before? Or did he simply not like being taken for granted and had gotten himself in a snit about it?

Argh. Boys.

After returning the boat—none the worse for wear, thankfully—to the marina, we went out to dinner at a steak place Danyel wanted to try, and then zipped back uptown to the nine o'clock showing of the new Johnny Depp movie. I was happy to see that the star was taking time off from big pre-sold franchises and going back to his quirky, indie-house roots.

All of which meant, of course, that there wasn't a single moment to talk privately with Kaz.

Sunday morning we all went to Sol and Malika's church with them—a totally fun experience where the singing and worship were like a shout to the Lord. Very different from the clapboard church out in Marin where Gillian and I usually went, even though my dad wasn't renting the house out there anymore. We still liked it.

And then suddenly we were all saying good-bye, and I was no closer to getting to the heart of Kaz's problem than I had been on the grass at the marina. We stood on the curb outside Sol and Malika's house, waving as Danyel's truck disappeared around the corner. I lowered my arm with a distinct feeling of anticlimax and loss. I'd missed my chance to do this live, so now I'd have to do it over the phone or over e-mail, both of which presented a problem: it was way too easy to misunderstand someone or take what they said the wrong way. Not that I wasn't good at doing that in person, too, as Gillian could attest.

We said our good-byes to Danyel's sister and her family,

and before long the three of us were climbing the stairs to the dorm wing.

"I'ma go see how far Carly got on the dress," Shani said. "See you guys at supper." The click of her Sunday heels receded up the staircase.

In our room, Gillian scrabbled in her desk for her phone. I didn't really want to talk about Kaz with anyone but him, and besides, it looked as if she had other things on her mind. Maybe I'd go for a walk and let the breeze blow a clear direction into my head.

I changed into more comfortable shoes and strolled across the playing field, in maiden meditation fancy-free.

"Lissa!"

Or not. I turned to see Derrik, in jeans and his soccer jersey, jogging across the grass toward me. I realized belatedly that they'd probably played early this afternoon.

"Hey, Derrik. How'd you do?"

"Creamed 'em five to two. We played Collyer Academy. I thought you might have watched."

"Sorry. We had friends in from out of town and went to church with them."

He fell into step beside me, his stocky athlete's form giving me the next best thing to a sunshade. I'd forgotten to put on sunblock anyway. "You look nice."

Whoa. *Danger, danger, Will Robinson.* "Thanks. I haven't changed from church yet. I guess you have to miss worship when you play, huh?"

"Depends on the schedule. Today I did. Next week should be okay. Where do you go?" I told him, and his eyebrows rose. "All the way out there?"

"We like it. We know the people and I love the pastor. Solid teaching is what I need, and that guy delivers."

Silence fell, and I wondered if he planned to go all the way around the block with me. I hoped not. How was I supposed to figure out the Kaz situation with Derrik doing his looming thing on my left?

"So, we got interrupted the other night."

It took me a second to remember what he meant. "I'm sorry about that. I'm such a klutz sometimes." There had been no fallout from Ashley Polk at our committee meeting on Friday, so I'd concluded that stupid camera-phone picture had not been made public.

"What I wanted to ask you was, do you have a date yet for the Cotillion?"

An honest question deserved an honest answer. We had prayed together, after all. "I thought I did, but it turns out I don't."

"Do you want to go with me?"

"I. Um." *Great, Lissa. Way to sound mature.*

He had the nicest smile. "I know it's kind of a surprise, but I like you. We go to prayer circle, and I've seen you in the bleachers, so I thought you might like me, too."

Oh, dear. Time to find a new place to study.

"I do like you, Derrik. But it's a leap from bleachers to ballroom, you know?" Not to mention I needed some time to suss out Ashley on whether she'd put out a contract on my head if I changed my mind and said yes. "I'm the senior consultant for the whole gig, meaning I'll be spending a bunch of time making sure all the logistics work out and acting as emcee and doing crisis control. Not your average date, in other words."

"As long as I get a couple of dances, that's fine with me." His eyes were blue, not dark brown like Kaz's, but the smile reached all the way into them. "I'm pretty good at crisis control. Maybe I could even help you out."

"I'll let you know this week, okay?"

He hesitated. "You don't know right now?"

Which made me feel totally blond, like I couldn't make a simple decision. "There's something I have to work out before I can say yes or no."

"Like what? An offer from another guy?"

With a snort, I said, "Hardly. Trust me on that one. It's something else."

He waited a moment, as if expecting me to give him more, but I couldn't say a word without breaking Ashley's confidence. Finally he said, "Okay. Whatever. I guess I'd better go do something about my English paper. It's supposed to have five thousand words and right now it only has fifty."

"As long as they're fifty good ones."

He laughed and jogged away. Okay, so he hadn't liked being stalled, which was understandable, but he was still nice, offering to help me work the party. I mean, if Kaz wouldn't take me, and Derrik hadn't asked Ashley, what was to stop me from going with him?

Besides my confused and unreliable heart, I mean. And the memory of Ashley's face when I'd told her Derrik was in no danger from me.

"Lissa!" I'd reached the halfway point of the huge quadrangle of streets that formed the Spencer campus boundary when I heard a girl's voice half a block behind me. I turned to see Vanessa jogging up the sidewalk.

"Are you supposed to run?"

"Doc says exercise is mandatory," she panted. "Boy, you walk fast."

"Long legs and crowded brain. Which doc? Vallejo?"

"No. My obstetrician at UCSF." She gave me a look

under her lashes. "See? I do have the capacity to make smart decisions."

"I never doubted it. It was your timing that was worrying me."

"Well, you can stop worrying. About that, and about the abortion."

I let out a long breath on a one-liner of thanks to God, and before I could stop myself, I'd turned and hugged her. Both of us stepped back, surprised.

"Don't go getting all emo on me," she said in disgust. "I was never going to do it, you know. I was just playing with you. Which I guess was kind of lame of me. You were so cute, trying to convince me to do the right thing."

"I'm not going to lie about how relieved I am." So she'd been playing with me, huh? I decided to let that go. I could just hear Gillian saying *I told you so.* "What brought on this smart decision in the first place?"

"Something you'd probably understand. . . . This weird God thing."

Okay, that stopped my brain function completely. This was obviously my weekend to have jaw-dropping bombs fall on me.

"My mom's side of the family is this huge Italian Catholic clan, and I was brought up Catholic, like Brett Loyola. We both stopped going to mass around the same time, when we were thirteen or so. But I guess some of the stuff sank in over the years, the thou-shalt-not-kill and all that."

"It would be hard to live with the guilt if you'd gone through with it."

"Guilt has never bothered me," she said with a dismissive wave. "That's for people who care too much about what others think."

Uh, okay. It seemed to me she cared quite a lot about what others thought these days, especially when they were catcalling her in the corridors. But I didn't want to stop the flow, so again I kept quiet.

"Anyway, I've been talking with the counselor ad nauseam . . . literally. There's stuff about my mom that played into it. I am *so* not going to be like her in any way." Her tone dropped into harshness, and then softened. "So between that and your nagging, I tried to do the right thing."

After a second of impulse control, I asked, "What about the baby's dad? What are you going to do about that?"

"One thing at a time."

"He deserves to know, Vanessa. What if he wants the baby?"

A laugh burst from her. "You're kidding."

Nobody likes to be laughed at. I'd controlled my tongue for long enough. "Well, if you think so little of him, why'd you sleep with him?"

Again the laugh, but it sounded more for show than because she meant it. "The obvious reasons, you ninny."

"Don't call me names. Help me understand."

"For one thing, he's gorgeous."

"That goes without saying."

"You think I pick them only for their looks?"

"If you don't think he'd care about his own kid, that's a logical conclusion."

"Harsh, aren't you?"

"Honest."

"You can say that because you don't know him. He's amazing. His family are the landscape architects for our villa in Italy."

"So you did sleep with the gardener's son, like everyone

says." And here I'd thought the rumor mill was just being nasty.

"No, Lissa," she said in a surprising display of patience. "I mean he's the heir to one of the foremost landscape design companies in the country. They specialize in the equivalent of National Trust houses, from the seventeenth and eighteenth centuries. Pietro can design a garden you'd swear had been approved by Louis Quatorze."

"Oh." I regretted the residual cattiness that had made me share the gossip. "He sounds very talented."

"He is." Her tone softened as we rounded the last corner and the school gates came into view in the distance. "He's talented and beautiful and five years older than me, and my mother would have a pink furry fit if she ever found out about it. She has the same view you did about the gardener's son."

"Your family still doesn't know?"

"Please." She made a face. "The Principessa di Firenze would never live down the shame. Of course, the fact that she's paid a fortune in hush money about the two babies she aborted that aren't my father's or my stepfather's will never come up in *that* discussion."

I swallowed carefully. Imagine facing this kind of battle on two fronts—between your church's views, which you'd come to believe were right, and what your own mother obviously thought was expedient. And this was the maternal example Vanessa had to look up to? Yikes.

"I didn't know your dad was still alive," I said lamely, for lack of anything else.

"He isn't. He died in a speedboat crash when I was nine. I still miss him, every single day."

I couldn't imagine losing my dad. The very thought made

a chill run through me. "If it's a boy, you could name him after him."

"No point in that if I'm giving him up for adoption."

"Listen to us, talking as if it's a boy."

"It is," she said. "I had an ultrasound, too."

Oh, my. First she felt him swimming inside her; now she knew what he looked like. "That's going to be tough, giving him up."

"I know."

"You should tell Pietro."

"I know."

"He deserves the chance to be part of the choice, too, especially if he's as lovely inside as you say."

"I know. Can we not talk about this anymore?"

We'd reached the gates anyway. A breeze had sprung up, coming up the hill off the water. It felt good, cooling our backs, but it snuck under her white Aquascutum topper and blew it open from below. She shivered, and from behind a tree, a shutter snapped.

Vanessa cursed and snatched the coat closed around her. "I hate those people. Why don't they get a life?"

"We should have come in by the rain tunnel."

"I'm glad I wore a coat, at least. And I had my hair trimmed yesterday."

This sounded so much like the old Vanessa that I had to smile. "Talk to you later," I said. "I'm going to go find my roommate."

She nodded and pushed open the front doors. The fact that she let them swing shut in my face didn't even faze me. She might be willing to confide in me, but she was still Vanessa.

Some rules didn't apply to her.

chapter 17

AS DINNER WRAPPED UP, I caught Ashley Polk's eye at the next table and waved. "Want to get dessert and join me?" I mouthed, pointing at the toothsome display of ganache-covered chocolate layer cakes across the room.

Her face went blank and she motioned vaguely to her ear. What did that mean? She turned away and began to talk to someone else.

Hmm. Maybe I'd been too optimistic about the cell phone picture. I hadn't been around all weekend—anything could have gotten out to cause trouble. Well, public or not, I wanted to clear the air between Ashley and me, which would then clear the path to Derrik and me, if that was meant to be.

Derrik and Lissa. Didn't that sound weird? Clunky, like a car with a flat tire. Not smooth, like *Kaz and Lissa.*

But that was stupid. There was no Kaz and Lissa, and never had been. No pair. No couple. Just friends, circling around each other independently. Not a bicycle. More like a gyroscope, with wheels inside wheels.

Never mind. Focus.

I abandoned dessert (with less than a month to go until Cotillion, it was time to knock off the sugar and bump up the water and fruit intake, anyway) and dogged Ashley out of the dining room. She moved in a circle of juniors, some of whom were on the Committee, who would probably take over the table in the window next year after we had graduated and were out of the way.

If I were a freshman, I'd find some of them intimidating. Livvy Valentine belonged to a powerful Silicon Valley venture capital family who had financed the startups of many of the students' parents. Dorian Escobar's mom was dating George Clooney—one reason parental visits had waned this term. Two of the girls were Gettys and one was a Hilton.

And at this moment all of them were ignoring me. "Ashley, wait up."

She turned, her eyebrows raised in surprise. "Did you say something?"

The other girls moved on a few steps, enough to give us the illusion of privacy while being able to hear every word.

"Can I talk to you a minute? Privately."

"I don't think there's anything left to say, Lissa."

"Is something wrong?"

"Not for you. Why should you care?"

"If it's what I think it is, your information is bad. That's what I want to talk about." I opened one of the waiting rooms outside one of the administrators' offices. On Sunday night, it was empty. "Alone, okay?"

With an annoyed huff of breath, she rolled her eyes

toward her posse. "I'll catch up with you guys in the common room. Mommy wants to give me a talking-to."

Oh, please. The girls giggled as they walked down the corridor, their Louboutin and D&G heels tapping out a message that told everyone, "We have it all and there's nothing left for you." I felt sorry for next year's students.

Inside the waiting room, Ashley leaned on the door, her whole body informing me I was a waste of her valuable time and she had somewhere way more fun to be.

"It looks like you've seen a certain gossip-gram picture."

"What if I have?"

"It explains this sudden change. I thought we were friends."

She dropped the pose and leaned forward, her temper snapping between one second and the next. "You promised! You told me you weren't interested in Derrik, and the next thing I know, you're plastered all over him!"

"It was an accident."

"Give me a break."

"It was. Ashley, listen. I tripped and fell on him at the vending machine and some trashmonger snapped the pic. You know how they are. They may as well be standing out at the gates with their cameras. Some kids get a thrill out of spreading stories that aren't true."

"So you can look me in the eye and say you're not going out with him?"

I could, and did. "I'm not going out with him. But—"

She wilted against the door. "Oh, thank goodness."

"He asked me to Cotillion."

Slowly, her knees straightened. "No. You didn't just say that."

"This afternoon. That's why I wanted to talk to you."

She gazed at me, her eyes bleak as a winter's day. "What's it got to do with me? He asked you. Game over."

"I don't think he knows you like him."

"So? That won't make any difference now."

"But there's more to it than that. Sure, I'd like a date to Cotillion, but—"

"You said you had one."

"I was wrong."

"How can you be wrong about that?"

"Long story. The thing is, it's more important to me that you and I can work together. The dance needs to go off without a hitch, and I need all our teams pulling together, not the glossy posse making smart remarks in the halls and playing I'm-more-popular-than-you." Her gaze faltered. "It would be pretty stupid of me to go with Derrik, wouldn't it, knowing that it would hurt your feelings and ruin the Cotillion for both of us. Not to mention everyone around us."

I heard my own voice and realized I had just told myself the truth.

If Kaz didn't want to take me, I was going to go stag. I would do my job as senior consultant as brilliantly as I knew how. I would snag that A in Public Speaking. And I'd resist the temptation to take Derrik away from Ashley, because I wasn't the needy person Callum McCloud had once accused me of being. I didn't need the security of a date with a consolation guy to make myself feel better about being turned down by the one I really wanted. I could face a dance floor alone if I had to. After all, Gillian was in the same boat. If worse came to worst, we could get out there and shake it together.

"You would really do that?" Ashley's tone was returning

to its usual warm but businesslike self. No snottiness. No freezing disdain. "Turn a guy like Derrik down for the sake of school?"

"Not school. I don't want to stab you in the back. Don't get me wrong—Derrik is the nicest guy, and if circumstances were different, I'd probably tell him yes. But you and I were friends first, and I meant it when I said I wasn't into him that way."

She gazed at me. "You are so mature."

I couldn't help it. I laughed. "I wouldn't call it that. So . . . when I talk to him, do you want me to tell him you'd go with him?"

Color seeped into her face. "I'm not going to beg for a date. If he doesn't see me, he doesn't, that's all. I can still ask him to dance even if he does take someone else."

An idea brushed through my brain. "When's his next game?"

"Tuesday at four, at home," she said without even a glance at her planner.

"Tell you what. Let's go watch it together. You be your normal cheering self, and I'll make myself invisible. You know how guys are. He's going to notice the girl cheering for him, not the one doing her history homework."

"You think so?"

"I know so. Come on. Your friends are probably thinking we've killed each other in a cat fight."

"Don't worry about them." She opened the door and motioned for me to precede her. "You know what? I skipped dessert. Think there's any of that ganache left?"

The improvements to my diet would have to wait until tomorrow. "Let's go find out."

Chocolate: The glue that holds women together. It was

nice to know there were things in this world you could still count on.

ON TUESDAY NIGHT at prayer circle, Gillian nudged me and leaned close. "What's up with Carly?"

I dragged my attention from what I needed to say to Derrik Vaughan, who had just taken a seat two people away from me, and focused. Good question. Across our circle, Carly's head was bowed, as if she were getting her spirit together before praying. But was it the overhead lighting that cast those dark circles under her eyes, or something more serious?

"She's been putting in a lot of hours on the dress," I whispered back. "She even got a night pass from the dean to work after lights-out."

"There's more to it than a few late nights," Gillian said. "Notice who's still not sitting beside her."

Brett had not come in with Carly, nor with Derrik. Had it only been a week since he'd shown interest in becoming a Christian? How toxic a week had it been: Carly and Brett weren't talking, Gillian and Jeremy had broken up, and Kaz had turned me down. All I needed to hear now was that Shani and Danyel were fighting, or that Alasdair had gone to join the Foreign Legion instead of getting a summer job in Inniscairn to be close to Mac.

Don't let that happen. I'm not superstitious, but I knocked on the wood of my chair just to cover all the bases.

After we'd all lifted each other up to God—Carly's voice only wobbled once, when she said Brett's name—and had sung the final praise song, I made up my mind. As people picked up handbags and backpacks on the way out the door, I made my way to her side.

"Sweetie, are you okay?"

"Yes." I could hardly hear her as she fussed with the clasp of her bag.

"Are you putting in a lot of hours on the dress?"

She nodded. "I'm leaving Thursday after school, and everything's done but the petal hem. I decided to put in an underlayer of silk chiffon so the skirt would split and it would look like a new flower unfurling with every step she takes up the aisle. But every time you make a design change, it means another muslin and more work."

"Do you need help? I'm pretty good at picking up pins."

At last, there was the Carly smile. "It's okay. I have a couple of sophomore minions who do that for extra credit. Technically I'm tutoring them in design, but it amounts to pin-picking a lot of the time. Or pressing seams. Or basting."

"Is it only the dress that's giving you the Vuittons under your eyes?"

"Does it show?" she asked plaintively. "So much for my new concealer."

"Only to people who know you. Gillian caught it first. And Shani's looking pretty worried, too."

Everyone had left the room, including Shani and Gillian, who'd telegraphed "Update us later" on their way out the door.

"At least Shani still has Danyel—" Her face crumpled and tears welled in her eyes.

I pulled her down into one of the chairs by the piano. "It's Brett, isn't it? What is up with that guy?"

"He can't get over me choosing FIDM over him."

I handed her a tissue from the new packet in my bag. With the week we'd had, I'd thought it best to stock up.

"Nothing I say makes any difference," she said through the tissue, and blew her nose.

"Would it help if I talked to him?"

"I don't know. Probably not."

"I can't stand to see you this way. The two of you belong together, like chips and salsa. Meatballs and tomato sauce."

"Who's the meatball?" came muffled through the tissue.

I took heart. "Him, of course. Anyone who doesn't worship the ground you walk on is a total meatball."

She mopped her eyes and I got half a smile for my efforts. "If you want to talk to him, I guess it couldn't hurt. He's pretty private, though. He might think you're butting into his business."

"I've had a lot of practice at that lately."

"What, with Gillian?"

"No. Vanessa. She's not going to have an abortion. That's something."

"So you're still friends with her?"

"I wouldn't call it that. But she needs to talk without being gossiped about or judged, and I'm there."

Carly was silent for a moment. "I think you're doing the right thing. Jesus said we should love and forgive. He was the guy reaching out to the tax collectors and that woman by the well at Samaria. People talked trash about them, and whispered about Him for doing it, but He still did it." She glanced at me. "People are whispering about you, too, but that's not stopping you. I think that's good."

"Let them. It's not the first time. And not doing what I think is right because I'm afraid of people talking is too junior high." I reached around her shoulders and gave her a squeeze. "If you can forgive your mom for doing what she thinks is right for her, then Brett can man up and forgive you for doing what you think is right for you."

Carly's brown gaze met mine. "That's what it boils down to, isn't it? We're all trying to do the right thing, and people get aggravated by it."

"I think Gillian sees my point of view, at least, and it's just her protectiveness talking most of the time." I got up. "Brett will come around. I'm going to find him right now, before I lose my nerve."

"You'll tell me after, right?"

I nodded. "Keep an ear out for your phone, in case I get back too close to lights-out."

I stepped into the corridor, and out of the corner of my eye, a big shadow moved behind the door. A second later I was glad I'd choked back a girly scream because it was only Derrik.

"Hey," he said. "I've been waiting for you, Obi-Wan."

I laughed and felt my heart settle back into its normal rhythm. Carly slipped out the door and headed toward the Life Sciences wing as Derrik fell into step beside me.

"You didn't go for coffee with the others?" I asked, and then wished I'd said something more intelligent.

"I just wondered if you'd made up your mind about Cotillion, that's all. You said a couple of days."

So I had. If last week was Toxic Week, this was shaping up to be Fallout Week. "I have made up my mind. I would have loved to go with you—" He began to smile, and I finished in a hurry. "But I can't."

"Oh." His brows knit in a frown. "Did someone else ask you?"

Meaning did I get a better offer. I couldn't let him think that. "There isn't anyone in this school I'd rather go with than you. But . . . can I be totally honest with you?"

"I hope so. Being as we pray together and all." His gaze on mine was so level and grounded that I wished once more my answer could be different. But I was done grasping at people to help me get what I wanted. I could stand on my own two feet.

Even if it meant standing all by myself.

"The truth is, there's more to this than a date to Cotillion. Someone out there really likes you, and if I go with you, I'll have broken my word to her. See, I told her I wouldn't."

"You did." He eyed me. "You told some random girl, and you made me wait until now for the same answer?"

Oh, dear. "Derrik, please don't be mad. I didn't know for sure how upset she'd be if I said yes. But I know now. So that's what my answer has to be."

"I don't get you," he said gruffly. "Since when do you have to get permission from other people for a date?"

Obviously the whole "be loyal to your friends" angle was lost on him. Maybe he was one of those guys who wanted the facts, not the truth. So I played that card. "Besides the fact that she's my friend, I need her help on a project for one of my classes. If I don't get her help, I won't pass."

"This is really about a grade?" He sounded astonished.

I let him think so. "The grade is the end result of a long chain of events. And it all starts with you."

He thought for a minute; then his scowly expression brightened. "Guess I'm really important to you, then, huh?"

"Let's put it this way: I can't have a positive without you being the negative."

"So who's this certain someone?"

"I can't tell you. But if you keep your eyes open, I know you'll notice her."

"So someone likes me so much they'd blackmail you to get me?" He sounded pleased about this. I'd be creeped out, but I guess you have to take your compliments where you find them. Guys. Honestly.

"Not blackmail. But the possibility of failure is working just as well for me. I really want that grade, and two other people are depending on it, too."

"It's nice to know it's not me," he said.

"It's definitely not you," I assured him. "In an alternate universe, I would totally have gone with you."

"We can be friends, though, right? That certain someone won't have a problem with that?"

"I don't think so. And we're more than friends, Derrik. In God's eyes, you're my brother."

"I hope you don't mind having one dance with your brother, then." He slung an arm around my shoulders, surprising me for the second time, and gave me a squeeze. "Who was that girl sitting next to you at the game today? The one who went crazy when I made that big save?"

I kept a straight face and resisted the urge to punch at the sky and yell *Yes!* "The blonde? Or the Goth chick chewing on garlic tablets on my other side?"

"Uh. The blonde."

"Oh, that's Ashley Polk. She's, like, my right-hand girl for the Cotillion. Very together. Totally smart. Big soccer fan."

"Ashley Polk. Huh." We'd reached the stairs to the dorms. "See you tomorrow, Lissa. And thanks."

"For what?"

"Being honest. Not many girls in this school would skip the mind games and just lay it out like that."

I just smiled, gave him a wave, and headed toward the front doors. Honest, huh? Well, Derrik didn't know it, but he'd been my warm-up act in that department.

Because now it was time to talk to Brett Loyola. Time to set the honesty for stun.

chapter 18

MRS. LOYOLA IS one of the nicest women I know—the kind who makes sure there's a plate of cookies lying around when her son's friends come over, or the kind who gives you a bed and some breakfast when you need them (which I know from two personal experiences). She ushered me into what used to be the parlor when this house was first built in Edwardian times, but which was now a TV and Wii room.

I thought she'd go holler at Brett and tell him he had company, but instead she hesitated as I took her invitation to sit on the squashy leather couch. "Lissa, is it—I mean, do you know what—" She stopped and took a breath. "Is Carly all right?"

Honesty time.

"That's why I'm here. Brett won't let her talk to him, so I came to see if I could help."

A long breath rushed from her. "You girls. I'm so glad she has friends like you. Brett hasn't been himself and I

173

know he's miserable, but he won't talk to me, either. It's so frustrating because since he met Carly, our relationship has been much better. It's like going back to square one from a year ago."

She gazed at me as though one little conversation would solve all her problems. That was a pretty heavy burden for me to carry.

"He might not talk to me, either, Mrs. L."

"Tell you what. He doesn't know you're here, because he and Tate DeLeon had World War Three going in his room. Tate left a few minutes ago, so he's not expecting anyone. Why don't you go up and surprise him? If I try to get him to come down here, he'll refuse and probably duck out the back."

"Deal. If I don't come out in half an hour, send in reinforcements."

I climbed the stairs to his third-floor room. The door shook in its frame from the force of the video-game explosions on the other side, amped up to truly belligerent proportions by a massive sound system.

Boys. Good grief. I was never complaining about Gillian's iPod again.

I opened the door and stepped inside, bracing myself to be blown against the wall by the sheer decibels. Brett had his back to me as he worked the joystick with his gaze on the huge plasma screen, sending a tank careening over a hill straight toward some kind of mud-brick building in a trackless desert. The partner joystick lay where Tate had left it on the floor behind him. Quietly, I picked it up so that when the bad guys lifted off in a helicopter from behind the building and blasted his tank, my tank raced over the hill and took it out with one well-placed tracer missile.

Brett whirled, his face a slack study in shock. "Where did you come from?"

"This is the thanks I get for saving your life?" The tanks trundled aimlessly, waiting for instructions, while the chopper burned in the sand.

"I thought Tate came back." He paused the game and silence fell, beating against my eardrums in a sudden withdrawal of sound.

"Nope, just me." I put a plate of chocolate chip cookies on the desk. "Your mom sent these up."

"No, thanks."

I took one and bit into it. Yum. Then I pulled a chair out and parked myself next to him. "They're great. You should try one."

"I know what my mom's cookies taste like. What are you doing here?"

I glanced at the DVD case. "Playing *End of Days?*"

"Funny. Carly sent you, didn't she?"

"No. I'm here on my own."

"Well, make sure you take another cookie for the road." He turned back to the screen and reached for the joystick.

I put a hand on his arm. "Brett. I have one thing to say, and if you don't listen to me say it, I'll start unplugging things from the walls, and then it'll get ugly."

"Touch my setup and your life is garbage."

"Can't be worse than your life right now." I took another cookie. They really were good. "I find it hard to believe that you like holding this grudge against her."

"I'm not holding a grudge. She made a choice. I accepted it. Now she has to live with it. Too bad if she doesn't like it."

"Nobody said it was an either/or choice. A binary decision. Black and white. You stay, I go."

"How do you figure that? She's going. I'm staying. You're going. Good-bye." Even though half his face was in shadow, I could hear the hurt etching his voice. He hunched, as if he thought I was going to attack him, and kept his arms in close. No quarter given.

I made myself more comfortable in the gaming chair, slouching a little and opening my arms in a direct contradiction to his body's argument. "It's a lucky thing I can empathize with how much you're hurting. Because the real Brett doesn't talk like this." I indicated him with the cookie to emphasize my point. "The real Brett, the one I'm friends with, respects Carly for standing up for what she believes is right for her. For not letting anyone redirect her life."

I let that sink in for a second and went on. "It's kind of like how she's rethinking her relationship with her mom. You know she's making a wedding dress for her?"

Brett shrugged and gave the screen, which had gone to sleep, a longing glance.

"The thing is, Alicia is doing what she believes is right for Alicia. And nobody can blame her for that. Who wouldn't want to marry a guy who adores her, even if he looks like Simon Le Bon? So there's Carly, accepting that, forgiving her mom for the past, and moving on, to the point where she's taking that dress on a commercial flight, SFO to ABQ, Thursday after school."

Brett shrugged with so little reaction that I realized he must already know her travel arrangements. Yet he did not speak. Hmm.

"So once she understands her mom, you can hardly blame Carly for doing what she thinks is right for Carly. Her dreams all begin and end in the Hollywood costuming industry. She'll do what she has to do to get there." My voice softened. "How can you punish her for that?"

"I'm not punishing her." Brett's tone had lost its combative edge, and the pain surging underneath began to leak through. "I knew we were going to different schools. I just thought we'd be close enough to see each other. I don't see what's wrong with that."

"Nothing," I said. "You guys are going to care about each other no matter where you go to school. What difference does it make where the schools are?"

"I need to see her," he said miserably. "Holidays aren't enough. She'll get busy on extra projects and meet new people and before you know it, a year will go by and she'll forget where I am."

"If you really think that, you don't know her very well," I told him. "She loves you."

The corners of his mouth turned down. "If she did, she wouldn't go tripping off to the other end of the state."

"Love doesn't depend on geography."

"What are you, a Hallmark card?"

"No. I'm her friend. One of several who hate to see the two of you so unhappy when you're meant to be together."

"I want to be together, too—right here. Too bad she doesn't."

"Does it have to be here?"

He frowned at me. "Um, yeah."

"Why? Didn't you get accepted at UCLA as well?"

"So? It's not Stanford."

"Does it have to be? Does your life depend on going to Stanford?"

"My family has gone there since it was founded. My great-great-whatever-granddad was friends with Leland Stanford back in the day."

"And you have to do what your family has always done? No choice? No hope? Just yes sir, no sir, off I go, sir?"

"No." He was beginning to sound nettled. Good. That meant I was bugging him, rocking his little world, and my work here was nearly done.

"Just asking." I snagged another cookie and got up. "By the way, I talked to Vanessa over the weekend. Did you know she's going to give her baby up for adoption?"

He nodded. "She says you're the only one in the school who will tell her the truth. Not that she likes it much."

That's me. Official truth-telling mascot for Spencer Academy. "If she brings it up, see if you can convince her to tell the father. Talk about giving a person a chance to do the right thing."

His gaze practically pushed me out the door. "You were leaving?"

"'Bye."

I closed it behind me, and immediately the sound levels inside came back up. Blam-a-ram! The panels and even the old-fashioned door handle trembled.

I had a feeling my tank had just been blasted to smithereens.

⟲

....

✉

To: gchang@spenceracad.edu
From: kazg@hotmail.com
Date: May 28, 2010
Re: Cotillion

So, Jumping Loon, now that you're a single woman, what are you doing about this Cotillion gig? As a single man, I just wondered. I told Lissa I wouldn't go with her on a "just friends" basis.

She's probably dazed and confused, but I just can't handle being taken for granted anymore.

I know I've bent your ear on that subject incessantly and I won't bore you any more, but I've been giving your green-eyed monster idea a lot of thought. Maybe I will come up with Danyel and see if it'll work. Something has to change the way she sees me, and you might be right. This could be it.

At the very least, we could herd together. Safety in numbers and all that. We can do like the musk oxen do and form a tight circle, facing out, while we dance.

What do you say?

Kaz

NOW THAT BART ran all the way out to the airport, seeing Carly off was just a matter of juggling luggage and buying a ticket from the dispenser in the train station.

"Are you sure your dad will meet you in Albuquerque?" Shani snapped the handle of Carly's carry-on roller out to its full length. Carly carefully bent the garment bag containing the dress over her arm while Gillian and I trailed her off the train platform and down to the walkway that would take us through the international terminal and over to the domestic terminal's ticket counter.

"Yes," Carly assured her. "It was just easier for him and Antony to leave from San Jose. Our flights arrive within twenty minutes of each other, so it's no big deal."

"Don't tell me your dad's going to the wedding," Gillian said.

"Not hardly. He may be ready to move on, but I don't think he's ready for that. He has some business meeting set up on Saturday, but in the meantime we're all staying in a suite at the same hotel."

We approached the ticket counter and Carly carefully handed me the garment bag. I was so afraid of crushing its contents that I held it in the air instead of putting it over my arm.

The ticket agent scanned the barcode on Carly's e-ticket and frowned at the screen. "You're traveling this evening, miss?"

"Yes, flight 638 at five fifty, into Albuquerque at nine thirty-five."

"Under this name? Carolina Aragon?"

"Yes." Carly's voice sounded calm, but her face had paled. "Is something wrong?"

"I'm afraid there's no reservation here for you."

"But I have a confirmation number right here."

"It's been cancelled, miss."

"How can it be cancelled?"

"If you have the number, you can go online and cancel."

"But I didn't. I have to get my mother's wedding dress to her by tomorrow. She's getting married on Saturday!"

"Would you like me to see if there's a standby seat?"

A cold feeling of horror trickled through me—I couldn't imagine how Carly felt.

"I want the reservation I paid for! I even chose the seat closest to the first-class closet so I could keep an eye on my mom's dress!"

Gillian reached into her handbag and pulled out the slender Marc Jacobs wallet where her Platinum Visa and Gold AmEx lived. "Carly, don't panic. I'll buy the—"

"Carly?"

All four of us whirled at the male voice. Brett, dressed in jeans, an open button-down over a T-shirt, and a rumpled suit jacket, rammed his hands into his pockets and hunched his rower's shoulders in a pose I recognized.

"What are you doing here?" Carly looked as though his appearance was the last thing she could deal with right now. "I don't have time to talk. My flight just got—"

"I know. I cancelled it."

We must have looked like characters in a comedy. All four of our mouths dropped open.

"You rat!"

"What—did you hack the airline server?"

"Brett, that is going too far, even for you."

Carly just burst into tears.

Brett ignored the rest of us and only had eyes for her. "I'm in your family e-mail group, remember? You cc'd me by mistake when you made the reservation, so I had the confirmation number. Because the deal is, we need to talk, and you're leaving, so my dad lent me the company jet. It's going through preflight as we speak."

Again with the dropped jaws. Maybe we were in a movie. Any minute now the director would step out from behind a pillar and say, "Great shot, talent. You really nailed the goggle-eyed shock, there."

Carly hiccuped and I handed the garment bag to Gillian. I fished a tissue out of my bag and gave it to her.

"I don't understand," she said thickly.

"I'm flying to Albuquerque with you. I'll spend the whole trip groveling if you want. But after that, I hope you'll forgive me for being such a butthead and let me escort you to your mom's wedding."

Carly scrubbed at her face. "You cancelled my flight. You scared me to death!"

"I'm sorry. But I couldn't let you fly away without having the chance to make it right." He spoke as if the rest of us—the airport bustle, the requests for people to go to the white courtesy phone—didn't exist. As if he and Carly were the only two people standing there on the concourse. "You're so good at doing the right thing. I guess I need some coaching."

"You sure do." But she was softening.

In his pocket, his phone pinged. "That's the pilot. They're ready for us. We still need to go through security, but there's a separate boarding area for private planes."

Without a word, Shani rolled the suitcase over and tilted the pull handle smartly into his hand. Carly held out her arm, and Gillian gently laid the dress over it. "Good luck," Gillian said. "Send pictures."

Shani kissed her on the cheek, and I gave her a hug, careful not to bump the bag. As the two of them walked away to join the security line, I swallowed my surprise—and the lump in my throat. Doing the right thing wasn't easy sometimes. But it was sure easier when you had a little help from your friends.

And it was kind of nice to know that my tank hadn't died in vain.

TEXT MESSAGE

Lissa Mansfield	Kaz, you there?
Kaz Griffin	I'm here.
Lissa Mansfield	Is your ringer off?
Kaz Griffin	Wasn't sure whether to answer.
Lissa Mansfield	?? Can we talk? I'll call your cell.

chapter 19

FALLOUT WEEK BEING almost over, I figured it was safe to call Fallout Boy and have it out with him. After all, I'd solved the Derrik problem without hurting his feelings too badly, and from the rapturous text messages all of us had been getting from Carly since she and Brett landed in New Mexico the previous night, things were looking up on that front, too.

There was nothing I could do about Jeremy and Gillian, and I could only open up the di Amato Landscape Design and Restoration Web site in Italy to gaze at Pietro di Amato's headshot so many times.

Yes, curiosity had gotten the better of me, and there he was, right at the top of the Google search. The man, as Vanessa had hinted, was jaw-dropping, breath-stopping gorgeous. Poster-worthy. In fact, someone should really make a fifty-foot banner and hang it from the roof of the Uffizi Gallery, because he totally deserved to be commemorated along with the less perfect creations like, oh, Michelangelo's *David*.

But I digress.

Because under his headshot was an e-mail link to contact him, and I can't tell you how many times my cursor hovered over it—clicked it, even, to bring up a mail screen that I immediately deleted. Yes, I know what you're thinking. It was not my place to tell the man he had five-ninths of a son over here in California. Maybe he was the uninvolved father to Vanessa's anti-Madonna and had no interest in the baby at all.

But still my cursor hovered.

Calling Kaz was a relief. At least I could act on that. Gillian and Shani were out at the field watching the soccer game—which seemed to be going well for our team, judging from the distant happy shouts that floated through our dorm room window every few minutes. I had time and privacy, both valuable commodities when you were having a heart-to-heart with your BGF.

"I can't believe you guys don't have classes Friday afternoons," Kaz greeted me. He never said hello like a normal person. With him and me, it was more like an ongoing conversation anyway, interrupted at intervals by classes and other obligations. At least, that was the way it used to be. Now the silences of real life seemed to be longer, and our conversations over text, mail, and phone shorter.

That needed to be fixed, stat.

"A perk of my privileged upbringing," I said in a smug Beverly Hills voice.

"Or your shortened attention span."

"True enough," I admitted. "Are you home or at the beach?"

"Home, getting ready to go to the beach. Danyel might remember to pick me up, if he's not yakking with Shani."

"She and Gillian are watching the soccer game, so he'll have to compete with Derrik Vaughan and his hot teammates."

"Athletes. Pah."

"Derrik's nice. He asked me to Cotillion."

Silence, while I pictured Kaz's head spinning on his neck. Heh.

"And you're not out there watching him because . . ."

"Because Ashley Polk wants him. And I told her I'd stay out of the way of true love because she's my friend."

"That was noble of you."

"If there's one thing I've learned, it's that you don't mess with your friends."

"Especially if they have connections with the video geeks." He paused while I blinked in surprise. "You told me about your big project. Or maybe it was Gillian."

"You make me sound like I have ulterior motives, you rat. But it doesn't help that she's the queen of the media lab and she can help me, Shani, and Vanessa tape the entire production process for our Public Speaking class. If I go to Cotillion with Derrik, none of that will happen, the three of us will fail Public Speaking, and Ashley will dismember me and feed my pieces to the seagulls at Fisherman's Wharf."

"Wow." He was silent for a moment. "Asking a girl to prom was never this scary in junior high."

"Oh, I think it was. It was just a different level of scary. Why, who did you ask?"

"Katie Fedorov. You remember, that girl who used to be your best friend? She said no and I came and cried on your shoulder. You told me to stop being such a weenie and lent me your sister's skateboard for a week."

"Ah, yes," I said, remembering. "That's when you broke your arm. I don't think your mom ever forgave me."

"Since she's not around anymore, it doesn't matter, does it?"

I kicked myself for bringing her up. Kaz hated talking about his mother, who had left him and his dad that summer to marry her wealth management advisor.

"So while we're talking about asking people out, how about you give me the real reason you won't come to Cotillion with me? We never got a chance to hash it out when you were here last weekend."

"Due to my clever time management skills."

"You dropped a bomb on me and then avoided talking about it on *purpose*?" I held the phone out and stared at it. Did I have a wrong number? Who was this person?

"Would you relax?" I heard his tinny voice say, and put the phone back to my ear. "Can't a guy just say what he's got to say and leave it at that, without having to present a paper about it to a committee?"

"I am not a committee. And when I get turned down, it's nice to have an explanation so I don't feel like a bag of trash that just got tossed in the Dumpster."

"Did you give Derrik the Soccer Player an explanation?"

"Of course. The same one I just told you, only I left out Ashley's name. She'll make sure he figures that one out on his own."

He heaved a sigh. A nontheatrical one. One that meant he was clearing the decks for bad news. *Danger, danger . . .*

"Okay. You want an explanation. Here it is. The only reason you asked me to Cotillion is because I'm convenient. Available. Currently unclaimed and unlikely to turn you down."

"That's not true. I asked you because you're my best friend and I want to share the big events in my life with my friends."

"Right. You told me that last weekend. But, see, what if I want more than that?"

"What does that mean?"

"What if I want to go as your date? Your guy. With the whole romance thing going on."

"You?" The second I said it, I wished I could grab it back. Insulting much? "I mean, we don't have that kind of relationship." What had I thought earlier? Oh, yeah. "We operate on a different level."

"Obviously you don't think I operate on the boyfriend level. With you." The life leached out of his voice.

"No, no. I mean, Gillian thinks you're hot and she's right. You are."

"That's not what I meant."

"What *do* you mean, then? I don't *need* a boyfriend, Kaz."

"See, that's exactly what I mean. You don't need another Prada bag, either. Or another iPhone. Or any other accessory."

The breath whooshed out of me. "You lost me. Can we go back to hello and take it from the top?"

"You see a boyfriend as an appendage. An accessory. Something you like to have around to take out on special occasions, but that's not totally necessary for every day. I want more than that. I want to be necessary."

"You *are* necessary. I think of things to tell you all the time. I want to see you whenever I can. How much more necessary can you be?" Then an idea occurred to me—one that had to be said. The elephant in the living room that he was too sensitive to bring up. "Kaz, is this about sex?"

"Oh, good grief." He sounded utterly defeated. "Goodbye, Lissa. Have a good weekend."

Click.

My best friend had just hung up on me.

THE LAST MONTH of senior year is supposed to be this triumphal ride to the finish, drenched in sunshine and victory and teachers easing up on homework.

I peered at the sky as I crossed the playing field, heading back to the dorm after Phys.Ed. Yep. Sunshine. Everything else? Not so much.

Not for me, anyway. Carly's life seemed to be back on track, at least. In the two weeks since her mom's wedding on Memorial Day weekend, she and Brett had become tighter than ever. In between fittings and festivities out there in New Mexico, they'd spent a lot of time talking, and by the time Alicia had become Mrs. Richard Vigil, Brett had made up his mind to register at UCLA instead of Stanford. How he managed to break this to his father, I don't know. But somehow I figured that Mrs. Loyola, weighing a Carly-less Brett going to Stanford versus a happy Brett going to UCLA, would use her influence to work on her husband's disappointment.

Since my disastrous phone call with Kaz, I couldn't seem to shake the regret and loss that hung over my emotions like a gray smog. In the mornings, I'd gaze at my yogurt and fruit, a sick lump in my stomach.

"Lissa, not eating isn't going to make it better," Gillian said after about three mornings of the same, but I just couldn't.

"Are we going to have to force-feed you?" Shani's tone was no-nonsense, but worry lurked in her eyes.

Not even the prospect of shopping for a Cotillion dress could pull me out of it, because if he wasn't going to be there, it didn't matter what I wore. Oh, I got one, don't worry. Gillian and Shani made sure of that, delivering me to Robin Brouillette's studio one day after school, where the designer made me a beautiful sky-blue confection with a rose-petal bodice that, under normal circumstances, would have had me babbling with happiness.

But circumstances weren't normal. I'd made an awful mistake and now I was paying for it.

How could I have been so stupid? That final click of the phone in my ear seemed to have set off an explosion of neurons all connecting at once in my brain. I'd handled the whole thing badly, had misunderstood everything he'd said because I was too mired in my own thinking to get what he was trying to say.

What was the matter with me? "We operate on a different level," I'd said fatuously, when that was the whole point. He wanted to take our relationship to a different level, and there I was, stuck in the way we'd been since elementary school. Well, I'd grown up in a hurry, hadn't I?

Even a flying trip to Santa Barbara the weekend before finals didn't do any good. Kaz's dad met me on the front porch of their house, his face slack with surprise.

"Hey, Lissa, I didn't expect to see you here. Have you graduated already?"

"No, not yet. I just thought I'd fly down to see my dad." I craned a little to look behind him into the Spanish-style living room. "Is Kaz home?"

"No, not right now."

"Will he be back before dinner?"

"I don't think so. He went eco-camping with a bunch of the guys. Something to do with their environmental science class, they said, but it's more to do with having fun and getting a Friday off school, if you ask me."

"Oh." I turned away, disappointment such a heavy weight that I could hardly keep my shoulders from slumping.

"Lissa, are you okay?" Mr. Griffin asked behind me. "Do you want to leave a message for him?"

"Um, no. It wasn't important. I just thought I'd stop by, since I was in town."

As I drove home, places we'd hung out in elementary school and junior high jumped out at me. The playground at Willows where he'd set me spinning on the merry-go-round and I'd tumbled off it and thrown up from dizziness. The pond in the neighbor's backyard where we'd watched tadpoles become frogs. The beach where we'd learned to surf and, later, where we'd sat up late and solved the problems of the universe.

Every place was so familiar, and yet . . . that was the problem. They were all scenes from childhood—something I'd left behind too late.

What was that line from *A Room with a View?* I'd quoted it myself in the term paper I had to turn in next Wednesday: "But to Cecil, now that he was about to lose her, she seemed each moment more desirable."

I was Cecil Vyse, the idiot. I'd pinned a bunch of my own childish notions all over Kaz and told myself that he was my friend. And why? Because it was safe. Because with Kaz, I'd never face the humiliation dished out by people like Aidan Mitchell and Callum McCloud, two guys who'd worn the label *boyfriend* for me. I'd kept Kaz in his place, and now that he'd burst out of it by speaking to me with total honesty, I'd tried to push him back in and lost him in the process.

I thought I was so mature. But it had taken this last couple of weeks, learning what loss really was, to make me finally grow up. Now I knew where the term *growing pains* came from. It had nothing to do with calcium deficiency, and everything to do with the mind and emotions.

How did people learn to live with this gray haze of "I'm sorry"? To realize how wonderful the other person was, and never be able to act on it?

"You've got to try to focus on something else," Gillian finally told me on Sunday, the first day of our last week of high school. "Agonizing over it and beating yourself up over what you said or didn't say isn't going to change anything. Trust me, I know."

We'd had the car drop us in Sausalito after church, and she, Shani, and I sat at a sunny table overlooking the Bay, drinking fresh-squeezed orange juice while we waited for our brunch orders to arrive.

"You and Jeremy are still friends, though," Shani pointed out. "Kaz won't even talk to Lissa, on the phone or in person."

"That doesn't mean I don't regret it," Gillian said.

"Jeremy would take you back," I told her softly. "I know he would."

"I know, too. But I can't. It would be like trying to surgically attach an arm you'd just removed."

Shani flinched. "Spare me the romantic images, girl."

"It took everything I had to say those things to him and make the break." Even a month down the road, the memory had the power to make her mouth tremble. "I can't go back and undo it. I have to go on. He goes to Davis and we go to Harvard."

"And we all go to the Cotillion wishing we were with the guys we've chased away." The thought of it overlaid the sunny day with gloom.

"Speak for yourself," Shani said briskly. "Y'all better not

have these long faces next weekend, or Danyel really will be chased away. And I'm not having that."

"This is all we have to look forward to?" I moaned. "Pity dances from Danyel and Brett? I knew I should have said yes to Derrik Vaughan when I had the chance."

"If you had, I'd have gone around you and broken it up," Shani informed me. "I'm not putting in all this work for Public Speaking and having you mess it up because you want a date."

She was right, of course. That boat had sailed, and Ashley Polk had been working her fingers down to nubs for us.

"I heard Ashley was going to Cotillion with him," Gillian said.

"Does Derrik know he was the prize in this whole exercise?" Shani asked.

"Oh, I told him," I said. "I didn't tell him who liked him, but when he didn't get why my friendship with Ashley would make me turn him down, I changed gears and told him my grade depended on me not going out with him. Boys are so weird. He thought that was a compliment."

"Guys love it when girls fight over them." The waitress put Gillian's plate down in front of her and she paused until we all had our food: fruit salad and Brie—the smallest thing on the menu—for me, an omelette and hash browns for Shani, and *huevos rancheros* with fresh *pico de gallo* for Gillian. "I don't see why. One guy is enough trouble. Having two fighting over me would make me run screaming for the hills."

"Jeremy wasn't trouble," Shani said softly. "He was lovely, as Mac would say."

"He was," Gillian agreed. "I'm glad we're still friends. I still plan to dance with him, mercy or not."

"Have you heard from Mac?" I asked. "Google Alerts sent

me a link to an article a couple of days ago about the big grand opening at Strathcairn happening in September."

"I got an e-mail last night," Shani said. "Their school year is over and she's back at the castle, 'working like a draught horse,' she says. Whatever that is. Carly would know. Anyway, she sent me pictures of the commercial kitchen they had put in. It's pretty amazing. And that *Naked Chef* guy from London is coming to open it on the big day."

"Jamie Oliver?" I asked. "He's cute. What's not to like about a guy who can cook?"

"Carly's invited over before college starts," Shani went on. "Wouldn't it be fun to go, too?"

"Why don't we?" Gillian knocked back her orange juice. "We can help them get things ready."

A long, Kazless summer stretched out before me. A few weeks in Scotland working like a draught horse sounded enormously appealing in comparison. "Suits me. I'll go. Shani, I'll pick up your ticket and Gillian can cover Carly's."

"Deal. I'll owe you."

"Of course you won't. It's a graduation present."

"Only five more days." Gillian sighed, chin on hand as she looked out over the sparkling Bay. "Can you believe it?"

"Five more days of backbreaking work and managing contractors and crisis control," I told her. "Five more days of wondering if we passed our finals and having to sit in class anyway." Five more days until I had to pack up my stuff and go back to Santa Barbara, where memories would ambush me at every turn.

"Five more days until Cotillion," said the only one among us who had a date.

Oh happy thought.

chapter 20

LIKE THE GLOWING EYES of Jawas, the camera lenses of the video geeks—sorry, the students from Media & Communications—followed me, my event coordinator, and my teams everywhere. I'm sure I actually heard groans of ecstasy on Thursday as the rigging crews arrived, unloaded the flying light bridge off the truck, and fixed the thousand-watt lights to it before the hydraulic lifters moved it into place. This wasn't a rock concert, but it was close. The event coordinator assured me that when the band arrived to do their sound checks Friday afternoon, all the structure work would be done, the lights would be ready to give us a club atmosphere, the draperies would be hanging from the walls of the ballroom, and the graduating class's banner would be raised in all its glory at the back of the stage.

The big picture was my job. I had a whole team for the tables and seating, and another for flowers and decorations, one for sound, one for the band. But the whole look, not to mention having everything come together by eight o'clock on Friday night, was on my plate.

Can you say "bunch-o-work"? But I was glad. The more I had to do, the less I had to think. If anything could save me, it would be not thinking.

The event coordinator and I were joined at the hip this week—or at least, joined at the ear via Bluetooth. Not for the first time, I realized how much hanging out with my mom at charity events had prepared me for a role like this. I was even issuing instructions the same way she did: pleasantly, with a smile, and leaving absolutely no room for argument.

It was a good thing that certain instructors—my English prof, the Phys.Ed. coach, my art teacher—had pretty much given us all a pass for the week, because I didn't have time to be in class. Some people, like Mr. Milsom, required that we be at our lab benches until the last minute of the last class of the last day. The guy was completely maddening. He didn't have anything new to say, and the juniors could have done all the cleaning and spraying that he assigned to us. I'm sure it was a power play, designed to squeeze the last bit of agony out of his victims.

Shani, Vanessa, and I managed to squeeze an hour out of Wednesday afternoon—the time normally occupied by Public Speaking, as a matter of fact—to storyboard our video on my MacBook Air. Once we had all the raw footage, Ashley would upload it to the school server and Shani and I would edit it with Final Cut Pro. Then it would go to Vanessa for the voiceover we'd already scripted, and by Sunday night, hopefully it would be done.

"I swear, if this doesn't get us all an A plus and a commemorative plaque, I'm going to hire a lawyer," Shani grumbled. "How can one class be so much work?"

"I should have gone with the group doing a poetry reading down at City Lights Books," Vanessa said. "One night, open and shut."

"And completely forgettable," I reminded her. "With this, you'll be watched by generations of grateful juniors."

She supported her spine with one hand as she stretched. "They'd better be grateful. If not, I'm coming back to haunt them all. And then I'll demand royalties."

When we got the storyboard done, Shani went back up to her room and I walked down the nearly empty corridor with Vanessa. Everyone who had any sense was outside on the lawn, or gone. I could have used some lawn time, myself. In fact, lying in the sun with an empty brain and nothing to do but turn over every hour seemed like the ultimate bliss.

"Come by my room, okay?" Vanessa said suddenly.

I blinked away my poolside fantasy. "Sorry. I was day-dreaming about having nothing to do. Sure. What's up?"

"I talked to Pietro. I thought you'd want to know." She clattered down the staircase and, even though I had a distinct feeling that something on the punch list was getting away from me, I followed. After a cliffhanger like that, wouldn't you?

She pushed open her door. "I finally got up the nerve to call him on—"

She stopped dead and I ran into her back. "Sorry. What's—"

I stepped sideways into the room to see a woman sitting on the bed. Dressed in a black suit—ohmigosh, Prada, from the last show in Milan, only she'd had the collar redesigned— and killer Balenciaga pumps, she rose slowly. Someday, if she allowed herself twenty years of dissipated living, plastic surgery, and petulance, Vanessa might look like this.

But I sincerely hoped not.

"Mama," she whispered.

The woman didn't answer. Instead, her hawkish black gaze narrowed on the plaid jumper Vanessa wore since skirts with waistbands were getting uncomfortable. Her daughter's hands moved to cover her belly, then hesitated and fell to her sides. "So. It's true."

"What are you doing here?"

"What does it matter? I came to see for myself. I could not credit even a photograph with showing me the truth."

"What photograph?"

But I already knew. The one from last week, when the wind had blown her coat open and the photographer's timing had been hair-trigger perfect.

"The one that was the centerfold of *Hello!* and *Paris Match.* The one that has disgraced us all."

Vanessa's throat moved as she swallowed. "It's got nothing to do with you."

But that stare had included me for the first time. "Whoever you are, you may go."

I glanced at Vanessa. I knew she was capable of holding her own against pretty much anything, whether it was an earthquake or a pack of raging juniors. But leave her with this woman? She scared me.

"This is my friend Lissa, and I've just invited her down here. Don't dismiss her as if she were a servant."

"That's okay," I whispered. "I'll just, um . . . We can talk later."

"Please don't. I'm sure Mama will be leaving shortly." She raised her eyebrows in the principessa's direction.

"I'm sure you do not wish to have this conversation in front of a witness."

"Lissa knows everything there is to know."

"Does she? Perhaps you could explain why it is that I do not. Why I must learn this dreadful news from *Paris Match*."

"Dreadful? Is that how you feel about your grandson?"

A spasm went over the woman's face, but whether it was disgust or distress, I couldn't tell. "Do not speak as though this is real."

"Oh, it's real." Vanessa took off her jacket and smoothed the fabric of the jumper taut, so that the mound of her belly was perfectly visible. "It's as real as it gets."

The principessa's nostrils pinched together as she turned her head away to gaze at the calendar hanging on the side of the wardrobe. Along with notes for doctors' appointments and assignments due, June 18 was circled in red pen. Graduation Day. Cotillion. The day after tomorrow.

"Do not be vulgar. Of course you must do something."

"I am, Mama. Thank you for asking. I'm eating lots of green vegetables and walking two miles a day and cutting out alcohol and coffee."

"And darn, you just keep gaining weight," I quipped, hoping to lighten the mood.

The basilisk stare pinned me in place. "Be silent."

"Mama, don't speak to my friends like that."

"I do not appreciate levity when I am trying to approach the solution to this difficulty. My doctor in London will take care of this. And once he has, you'll appear in public looking as you've always done. The regatta at Henley is in two weeks—that would be the perfect venue. We will demand a retraction from the magazines and they will have no choice but to comply."

I stared, translating this outrageous plan. Did she really mean what I think she meant?

"It's not safe to abort during the second trimester," Vanessa informed her. "Even you must know that."

"I certainly do know it, since I've experienced it. I nearly died."

And what about the baby? No chance there. Gulp.

The woman stared at me again. "I have your promise that nothing said in this room will leave it? Because if one word leaks to the press, I will know, and my lawyers will crush you and your family to pulp."

"Good grief, Mother." Vanessa sighed. "Lissa is the last person who would blab to the tabs. And her family is quite capable of taking your lawyers on. But that's beside the point. The point is, I'm not going to have your London abortion. I'm not going to Henley, either. I'm going to have the baby."

The principessa didn't miss a beat. "Have you arranged for a family to adopt it?"

"What if I haven't?"

"Then you will leave it to me."

"What if I don't want to do that?"

"Do not challenge me, Vanessa. You surely don't plan to keep this child and bring it up on your own? Because you will find that your trust fund will no longer be available to you."

"Fine. I still have the money from Grandmère."

"And that will provide you with a house and someone to care for the child?"

"If I'm careful."

"And your university career?"

"Might have to go on hold for a while."

Was she serious? The last time we'd talked, she'd been prepared to give the baby up. Had she changed her mind? I tried to picture a single Vanessa giving night feedings and buying groceries in the twenty-four-hour Safeway with a baby on her hip. Somehow I couldn't do it.

"You cannot possibly be serious." The principessa's tone held utter finality. "And if you are, I will not allow it. This mistake cannot ruin your life, or mine. I will not be the grandmother of the child of a gardener."

"He's half royal."

"He is not royal at all if he is illegitimate. Now. How soon can you be prepared to leave?"

"Mother, school isn't over yet."

"Nonsense. Your examinations are over, and you cannot plan to attend the graduation ceremony looking like . . . that."

"I certainly do. And the Cotillion on Friday night as well."

"No. You are coming with me. I have a car waiting outside. I'm sure your friend will help you load your clothes into it."

Unhurried, Vanessa picked up her blazer and hung it in the closet. "No. I'm going to enjoy my graduation, finish up my outstanding projects—which you have no idea about because you can't even be bothered to show interest in my classes—and go to Grandpère in Provence next week as planned."

"Does he know about this?" She gestured at Vanessa's middle.

"No. But it doesn't matter. He won't treat it like leprosy."

"Do not be so sure. He is, after all, the one who forced me to get my first abortion."

"Only because it wasn't his son's child."

At this point my brain slipped into complete paralysis. One thing I knew for sure: My parents might have their

faults, but at least they were normal. I was never, ever taking them for granted again. Can you imagine me having this
conversation with my mother? Now that I knew the kind of
raptor Vanessa had for a parent, the fact that she'd turned
out the way she had was . . . understandable. Forgivable,
even. How could you have a chance to develop compassion and empathy in your nature when your own mother
had aborted your half-siblings as thoughtlessly as she might
cough up some unpleasant phlegm?

She was phlegm. Nasty, toxic, and she didn't even smell
good. Had no one ever told her that Poison went out in the
eighties?

If this pregnancy caused an irreparable split between
mother and daughter, in my opinion it could only be a good
thing.

"Very well." The principessa rose. "You bring shame upon
yourself, and I will not stay to see it."

"I didn't expect you to."

Wow. It had never occurred to me that she would stay for
the graduation ceremony, either. I mean, can you imagine
having *that* perched on the lawn like a vulture during your
happy moment of academic triumph? Yikes.

"This discussion is not over. You may expect me at your
grandfather's by the end of next week."

"He won't let you in, Mama. He never does."

"I will not be alone."

With that, she brushed past us and went out. No hug, no
kiss, no "have a nice life." Vanessa closed the door behind
her and dropped onto the bed as if her knees had done all
they could and were giving up.

"I'm sorry you had to see that."

"I'm sorry you had to live it. What a harpy."

A huff of breath might have passed for a laugh. "I adored her when I was little. Always laughing, always so beautiful. She had flocks of men around all the time, like a court around their queen." Her voice trailed away.

"What happened? How did the queen turn into the wicked witch?"

She lifted one shoulder. "Life, I guess. The babies. After the second abortion she started to change. She's not a religious person, but maybe the guilt started to get to her."

"At least you won't have to live with that." I sat beside her. "Are you really going to have the baby and raise him on your own?"

This time the huff of breath had some humor in it. "No. I just said that to get her going. And to throw her off the trail."

"Pietro? You said you talked to him."

She nodded. Silently, a tear overflowed and trickled down her cheek.

"Here." Thank goodness the tissues were still in my bag. "Let it out, Vanessa. Just let it go."

With a gasp, she began to cry in earnest. I couldn't help it—I put my arms around her and patted her back while she wept it all out. Ten minutes must have gone by while I pieced together the broken bits of the story, muffled against my uniform blazer.

Pietro apparently had an older brother, Roberto. He and his wife had been through in vitro twice without success— and in an Italian family where he was one of three sons, this was extremely hard on the young couple, both emotionally and financially.

"So the brother is going to adopt the baby?" I said, trying to get it clear.

She nodded and slowly straightened. "You'd think it was a

gift from heaven. His wife—her name is Lisabeta—sent me an e-mail last night with pictures of the room they're planning for the nursery. It made me cry."

There had been a time when I would not have believed Vanessa *could* cry, never mind twice in one day.

"So even though you have to go through graduation, um . . ."

"Looking like a whale?"

"More like a porpoise. A sleek, really well-dressed one. But even though you have to do that, there's a blessing at the end."

"That's one way to look at it." She gazed into the distance for a moment. "In fact, that's the way I *will* look at it. This baby is desperately wanted—even if it's not by me. My job is to get him to his parents safely, isn't it?"

"Keep up those vegetables."

"I guess I'd better cave and eat the broccoli, then. I was holding out on that."

I gave her a hug. "You'll do fine. That baby will be the healthiest, most loved kid ever."

She looked at me for a moment as my arms fell away, and I braced myself for the inevitable Vanessa smackdown.

"I would never have gone through with this if it weren't for you," she said. "And Roberto and Lisabeta wouldn't be painting their nursery right now."

"You would have." I nodded almost to myself at my own certainty. "You'd have done the right thing."

"I'm not so sure. But you were. Why?"

Out of the fifty answers to that, I chose one. "Because I prayed about it."

"You couldn't have known it would turn out like this."

"Of course not. But God did."

She fell silent. I can feel the moment for a good exit, and I took it. As I slipped out the door into the corridor, I looked back. She was gazing into the distance again.

Maybe she was keeping those words and pondering them in her heart. I couldn't tell.

That was between her and God.

chapter 21

GRADUATION DAY!
Like *Christmas Day, wedding day, birthday*, those two words aren't just words. They're wreathed with flowers and float in the air.

Graduation Day! Woohoo!

And the best part? I didn't have to film, arrange, organize, or otherwise do one single thing during that part of the day except put on cap and gown and show up. After that . . . well, I'd think about that when I got there.

The ceremony was scheduled for two o'clock, and my parents and my sister, Jolie, arrived on the ten a.m. shuttle from Los Angeles. Since I could see the driveway from our dorm window, I managed to keep up a continuous surveillance starting at ten-oh-one. Finally a rented Beemer with its top down wheeled onto the gravel, and I think I set a land speed record going down the stairs, because I made it out the open front doors before Dad had even stopped the car. They piled out and the four of us crashed into a huge group hug, like one big happy organism with four heads and sixteen limbs.

Oh, it felt good to be with my family again! I mean, what a difference between this and the tête-à-tête with the principessa. I made a vow that instead of fighting over stupid stuff with my sister, I would appreciate her driving need to make a difference in the world. I'd love my dad for his skill as an artist, instead of feeling sorry for myself every time he had to fly off to the other side of the world for a shoot. And I'd find a minute to thank my mom for her unconscious training in event planning, because it was proving worth its weight in gold this week. No more whining because she put so much importance on charity. What else was it but a well-organized form of putting other people first?

"I'm so happy," I burbled when we finally split apart and could speak. "Seeing you guys here is like getting a big fat cake all to myself."

"With no calories," Jolie quipped. She was an inch or so shorter than I and she'd colored her hair a few shades lighter than her normal brown. My sister had also lost the last of the puppy fat that had driven her nuts as a teenager. She looked every bit the competent filmmaker she was going to be after one more year at UCLA Film School.

"Nice haircut, Jo," I told her. "When did that happen?"

"A couple of weeks ago. I donated it to Locks of Love." She shook it, and the neat wedge settled effortlessly into place. "This is a lot easier to take care of on set, especially in places like Morocco and Thailand."

"Grab your stuff and come on in." I motioned toward the door. "Dad, you know where the visitors' lot is, right?"

"I'll park it," Jolie volunteered.

"It's a stick shift," he warned as he hefted his and Mom's

matching weekenders out of the trunk and slammed it shut.

"I know, Dad," Jolie called as she ground the gears, wheeled the Beemer around, and shot off down the driveway. Dad winced and tried not to look back as he followed Mom and me inside.

"So how are you and your merry band?" Mom wanted to know as we climbed the stairs. "Ready for this to be over?"

"So ready. But you know what? All those years of watching you run events and helping Dad on set have really paid off. Producing the Cotillion is a challenge—and it's not over till it's over—but it wasn't nearly as stressful as I was expecting, thanks to you guys."

"Don't sell yourself short, L-squared," Dad said. "I'm surrounded by extremely competent females. You scare me sometimes."

I had to smile at his nickname for me, which stands for Lissa-love. He's such a softie.

"Better scary than scared," I said. "Here's our room. Come on in for a bit of calm before the storm."

"Where's Gillian?" Dad wanted to know as he and Mom sat on my bed, side by side. A happy little glow danced inside me at the sight of them. Even a few months ago, when we'd been together at Strathcairn for Christmas, I could do nothing but hope that they'd be able to figure out the distance that had grown up between them, including the trial separation that had frightened the life out of me. But something had happened at Strathcairn. I don't know what it was, but the fact that Mom's hand slipped into Dad's so instinctively as they sat next to each other now told me that any distance left between them was closing fast—and was maybe even gone altogether.

"Her folks are staying at the Four Seasons, and her aunt and uncle and cousins came up from the peninsula for a big family breakfast, so she's down at the hotel." I left out the fact that I had to talk her into going. Being locked in a hotel room with her dad isn't Gillian's idea of a good time. "I think they were going to the Top of the Mark."

"Lucky girl," Mom said. "Where are we taking you for lunch?"

"Downstairs to the dining room, if you want. I don't care where we go, as long as we're together."

As far as I was concerned, the food in the Spencer dining room was as good as any we'd find for a mile around, so that's what we did. And then Gillian arrived with her family, and it was time to put on caps and gowns.

"Black so suits me," Gillian said, turning in front of the mirror on the back of her wardrobe door. She wasn't entirely in black, though . . . the light and dark purple National Chinese Honor Society cord with its Chinese knots hung around her neck, as did her Harvard key. And under both lay a Dean's List stole like mine, in the Spencer colors.

"Not me," I said from the bathroom, where I was squinting at the mirror and trying to get my cap to stay on straight with bobby pins. Who even used bobby pins anymore, except for holding on mortarboards? "But hey, today I'll suffer with it just to get that diploma in my sweaty hand."

There. I slipped in the last pin. Nothing would carry this thing off my head except a gale-force wind, and it wasn't likely we'd see one of those in June.

"It was nice to meet your brothers." I walked out of the bathroom unnaturally straight, and pulled my gown out of its plastic bag. "And your dad seemed to be on his best behavior."

"He just closed a big funding deal before they flew out yesterday, so he's happy. I'll have to send the company a thank-you note." She pirouetted in front of me. "Any creases?"

"Nope. Me?"

"You're good. Ready?"

"I've been ready for twelve long years, girlfriend. Thirteen if you count kindergarten."

Laughing, we met Carly and Shani outside their room—both of them looking fabu in caps, gowns, and Dean's List stoles, and Shani in dangly diamond earrings that completely set off her sparkling eyes.

"Where did those come from?" Gillian wanted to know. "Rashid?"

Shani shook her head, making the twin diamond strings shimmy and dance. "Not every diamond in my life comes from him, you know. They're from the old days. I just haven't worn them in a long time."

"I wish Danyel could see you." *I wish Kaz could see me.* I pushed the thought away and whipped out my digital camera. "Come on, girls. Pose!"

So there in the light of the big windows over the stairs, we took pictures of each other—singly, in pairs, all together—every one of them showing us laughing, blessed in the power of our friendship, and most important, together at this turning point in our lives.

The bleachers had been turned into seating for parents and dignitaries as we got into a long line in alphabetical order and filed into our white chairs on the playing field. They announced the academic and sports awards first, and it was no surprise to anyone when Gillian won the Carrick Cup for the school's highest GPA and Brett won the Bill Walsh Trophy for Sportsman of the Year. There were a couple dozen civic awards and scholarships, one of which Carly won, much to her joy. It would put a dent in the tuition at FIDM—and that would make her dad even happier.

Tonight, during Cotillion, I'd have the pleasure of announcing the "social" awards, like service to the school and that kind of thing. I blocked it out of my mind. This afternoon I was going to enjoy being in the now at my graduation and not miss a single second worrying about all the work that lay ahead of me.

And then the student orchestra began to play "Pomp and Circumstance." We've all heard it a million times, right? But somehow it was different when it was me walking up there to the sound of my friends and family cheering, me shaking the dean's hand and receiving his congratulations (he, at least, remembered I'd come in second for the Hearst Medal), me feeling that rolled-up piece of paper tied with satin ribbons in blue, white, and gold.

It was enough to make me choke up.

But I didn't. Instead, I hollered "Yeeeehaaaaa!" and gave my parents the surfer's "hang loose" wave as I ran from the stage, a free woman at last.

Are you there, life? It's me, Lissa.
Ready or not, here I come!

"CATERING, CHECK IN."

"Dining room's ready to go, seating for five hundred is ready, and they're putting the last of the flowers on the tables." Summer Liang's voice came through my earpiece loud and clear. Away at the back of the ballroom, the florist moved from table to table. Summer was totally on top of her game.

"Doors open at seven."

"We'll be ready, Lissa. I can't wait!"

I disconnected and punched another number. "Sound and Stage, how are we doing?"

"Sound checks went fine at five o'clock," reported Tinker Davis. "One of the band's monitors fritzed out, so we borrowed one from the music department."

"Is an engineer from the rigging company still onsite?" *He'd better be.*

"Yes, he's here tying up some cables."

"Make sure he gets fed, okay?"

"Yes, Mom."

I grinned and signed off, then dialed my event coordinator. "Hey, it's Lissa. I'm in the ballroom doing final check before the doors open. Where are you?"

"*Where* is the valet service?" he snapped instead of answering.

"There isn't one. The signs are up pointing people to the guest lot." Wow, stress much?

"Lissa, we have to have valet parking for the VIPs."

"If they're VIPs, I'm sure they can read. Calm down, okay? The committee decided against valet parking months ago. All the seniors will be dancing and the juniors are too young to drive without an adult in the car."

"But—"

I cut him off with a quick rundown of my checklist, concluding with, "I'm going to go make sure all the awards got moved backstage."

"Has everyone who's getting an award been briefed? They'll be there, right?"

"No, they haven't. That's the point of doing it at the dance.

It's a surprise. Everyone in the school will be there, except for a few international students who left after graduation."

"That's crazy! What if your award winners are under the bleachers smoking dope when you call their names?"

"If that's the case, we have a bigger problem than their not showing up." I wondered how long this guy had been in the business. "Have you considered shots of vitamin B? Because your stress levels seem really high." He was creating stress where it didn't exist, but I couldn't exactly say that to him. He'd only redline, and then where would I be? "Try and have a good time, okay? I plan to."

When he disconnected, my phone rang again right away. "Ashley? I see cameras set up, but no operators. We want the final result of the teams' work before everyone starts coming in."

"They're on their way," Ashley reported. "The flower lady just left and that was our cue."

I left her to her job and made my way backstage. The old Edwardian ballroom had probably never seen the likes of the flying bridge, the miles of cabling, the lights and strobes that would give us our club atmosphere. Behind me, the band's instruments waited on stands, roadies still ducking and running as they did their own final checks. I made a mental note to ask Sound and Stage to see that they got fed as well.

In the anteroom behind the curtain, the silver boxes containing the awards were lined up on a table, in the same order they were to be presented after dinner and during the band's break. I'd do the first, and Shani would do the second, both of us filling our Public Speaking requirement. Ms. Curzon would text me, Shani, and Ashley the list of winners just before I was ready to present. The names would be as much of a surprise to us as to everyone, but Ashley's camera crew would have a few seconds to locate each winner and film them as they went up to the stage.

The boxes sparkled in the light, each one clearly marked with the award engraved on the statuette inside.

The Debate Club's Student of the Year.

The Values Award for the student who best exemplified the school's values of Loyalty, Purity, and Intellect—though how they were going to prove Purity I wasn't sure. Never mind. I'd just hand the thing over without comment.

Service to the School.

Board of Regents Honors.

Twelve boxes in all. I checked them off my list and headed out across the ballroom. T minus thirty and counting, and I wasn't even dressed yet.

I took the stairs two at a time and slipped into our room to find Gillian, Carly, and Shani in a last-minute state of chaos.

"These shoes aren't right," Shani moaned, lifting the hem of her Lagerfeld and regarding the silver pumps in the mirror.

"No one's going to see them," Carly said. "Not like this bodice. What was I thinking when I put this tulle pleating over it?" She tugged it up and slipped on a matching bolero jacket.

"You look beautiful, and Brett will tell you so." I kept my tone light and soothing as I dashed into the shower. When I got out, Shani and Carly were examining Gillian as she paced in front of two study lamps on the floor, turned to face up. "You can't see through it," I said over the sound of the hair dryer. "Even at two hundred watts you couldn't."

"I know, but ever since that *Gossip Girl* episode with the see-through dress, I've been paranoid." Gillian spritzed her hair one more time and slipped a spray of feathers on a clip into it.

"That's not from Tori Wu, is it?" I slipped into the strapless blue Brouillette and Carly zipped me up. "She usually amps up the trimmings more."

"Plain is okay, isn't it?" Gillian turned worried eyes on me, made even bigger by her skillful application of eye shadow.

"Of course it's okay. It's stunning. And that royal purple is perfect for you."

"That's what Jeremy said when I bought it," Gillian murmured, turning to locate her Jimmy Choos.

Ouch. I exchanged a pained glance with Carly.

"By the way, your parents left this for you." Gillian handed me a little box. "They said they'd see you at the dance."

I paused in the act of pulling off the pink ribbons. "Aren't they going to be at the dinner? I reserved places for all of us at the tables closest to the stage."

"While you were dashing around like a crazed person, Mrs. Loyola invited all our parents to their place for home-made ravioli," Carly said. "Would you turn that down for Dining Services, no matter how good their food is?"

She had me there. The parents would probably have more fun at someone's home, anyway, especially since Mom and Dad were staying there. Jolie had made arrangements to stay with a high school friend—she'd seen me graduate, but drew the line at coming to the Cotillion. "Posh as this place is, I'm never going to a high school dance again," she'd told me with a kiss and a laugh.

I opened the box to see my grandmother's Art Deco hair

clip with its sixty-two pavé diamonds. "Oh, my." Under it lay a note.

Darling,
*   Wear this and consider it yours. Your grandmother wanted you to have it, and I've been saving it for tonight.*
*   Love, Mom*

If anything could finish off a look, it was this, my favorite of all my mom's pieces. Shani, who has magic in her hands when it comes to hair, wound my long mane into an Audrey Hepburn pouf, and anchored the clip at the front so it looked almost like a tiny tiara.

"Girlfriends, we are ready," she announced, giving me a last mist of hairspray. "The guys are so not going to survive the sight of us."

"I hope they do," Carly said. "I'm planning to dance Brett's feet right off."

Gillian's phone chimed and she glanced at the text message. "They're here, right on time."

They?

"Who knew?" Shani said, leading the way out the door. "They only had, like, three hours to get ready and get over here."

"They who?" I asked.

But amid the laughter and clattering of expensive shoes, no one seemed to hear me. And the next minute I knew.

Standing in the entry foyer, Danyel turned to watch Shani come down the stairs. His smile lit up his whole face—almost to the point where you missed the fact that he looked dazzling in black tie.

And standing next to him was Kaz. He grinned up at us, too, and my heart flipped over in my chest.

He came. He really came, despite everything.

Wow, does he look fine in that tux.

He smiled at me as we took the last step into the foyer, alive now with the babble of excited students dressed in their best, with parents, with VIPs whose faces I recognized but whose names I couldn't remember.

And then Kaz looked behind me and stretched out his hand. Gillian took it and smiled up at him. "Ready?"

"Let's do this thing."

And then I knew.

Kaz had not driven six hours, rented a tux, and put on the pretty for me.

He was Gillian's date for Cotillion.

chapter 22

THE SHOW MUST go on. That's what they say, isn't it? No matter what happens, you've got to put on that smile and walk out there like you own the room, even if your heart feels like it's going to crack down the middle.

I think my heart did crack. I certainly felt shards of something in my stomach as we walked over the lawn to the ballroom in our finery, laughing and talking. Why hadn't Gillian said anything to me? When had Kaz asked her? She could have told me anytime in the last few days and given me a chance to prepare myself for the sight of them together.

To give her credit, she did give me a look or two as we seated ourselves at our table, as if to silently ask, "Is this okay? Are you all right?" But the simple fact that Kaz was sitting next to her and not me made it completely wrong. The universe was out of joint, and the discontinuity happened right there where their shoulders bumped.

I don't even remember what dinner was, after all the trouble my team had gone to in putting together the menu. All I could see was Kaz on the other side of the table, sitting next to someone who wasn't me. And what made it even worse? I'd brought this on myself by my own blindness. I hadn't woken up to what Kaz really meant to me until he'd given up and moved on.

I couldn't blame him for liking Gillian. All of us liked her. I loved her, for goodness' sake. She was brilliant and fun and they had the whole graphic art thing to bond over. They'd begun as friends, and it looked like things were going to progress from there. He and I had begun as friends, too. But because I'd been stuck in my own ideas like a dinosaur in a tar pit, I hadn't been nimble enough to adapt to change and climb out in time.

I was adapting now. In fact, as dessert came, the more I looked at them together, the more I felt like bursting into tears. Oh, they weren't indulging in massive PDAs or anything. Far from it. But were they holding hands under the tablecloth? Was that glance just a little too long, a little too absorbed? Did she like him more that he liked her? In the space of a few minutes I became obsessed about learning the answers, watching them out of the corner of my eye while I talked and laughed as if I didn't care.

"Hey, Lissa." It had taken until dessert for him to speak to me directly. How had our friendship devolved to this? "I got the revisions to *Demon Battle* this week. Nine single-spaced pages of stuff they want me to change."

"Yikes!" That was a lot of pages. "What's the matter with your editor? Is he on a power trip, or what?"

"Oh, no. It's a good thing. He wants more character stuff going on. Conflict in every frame—even the dialogue, not just the art."

"That'll make it a better story in the end, won't it?" Gillian asked, and Kaz nodded.

"Oh." Great. I'd just attacked a person he admired. Whereas Gillian knew just the right thing to say. Had she even read the book? Had she seen it when its very first sketches were only a dream on paper, like I had? Had she listened to Kaz's ambitions and hopes during long late-night conversations, like I had?

Did it matter? Kaz was moving in the present, not the past. And there I was, fading in his rear-view mirror. The girl he used to like. His childhood friend.

My phone gave its "you have a message" signal, and I pulled it out to see the list of award winners from Ms. Curzon. I pushed my plate away and took a fast gulp of ice water. "That's my cue, guys. Wish me luck."

"Luck," Kaz said.

"Warm up the crowd for me." Shani gave me a quick hug.

"This is your show." Carly blew me a kiss, Brett's arm around her shoulders. "Knock 'em dead."

Music began to play as I slipped up the stairs and into the anteroom to collect the first of the two trays of statuettes. Twelve little—

Wait a second.

Eleven? That wasn't right.

I counted again. There had been twelve boxes sitting here an hour ago. My glance flicked from the list on my phone to the printing on each box as I did a quick comparison.

Uh-oh. Service to the School was to have gone to Vanessa Talbot. But the box containing the statuette was missing.

There were only four people who knew the contents of the winners' list. Shani had been with me all through dinner. Ms.

Curzon had been entertaining the Board of Regents at their table to our left.

That left Ashley Polk.

The one who had fired Vanessa from the senior consultant job because her pregnancy would reflect badly on the school. The one who obviously had not changed her opinion about seeing the PeeGee Princess on stage, no matter how well deserved the award.

I hit autodial. "Ashley!"

"Right here. Comm and Media crews are ready to roll tape."

"Where's the Service statue? I'm backstage and there are supposed to be twelve awards. There are only eleven here."

"I have no idea."

"Ashley. This is no time for dramatic statements. Only four people have this list, and I've kept my eye on two of them all night."

"Are you insinuating that *I* took one of them?" Ashley's voice sounded dangerously cold.

Wait. Close mouth. Think carefully.

The Media and Communications students might be ready to roll tape, but they could pack it up and go dancing instead, at the drop of a hint. And then where would Shani's, Vanessa's and my grade and our project be? Not only that, I'd seen how Ashley could flip from friend to foe in moments. I'd far rather close out the year with a friend.

"Of course not," I said at last. "I just wondered if you or any of your crew saw anyone come in here since we set up, that's all."

"No, we haven't." Her voice had returned to its usual cool professionalism. "What are you going to do?"

There was only one thing to do. "I'll deal with it. Thanks, Ashley."

I disconnected. How weird. My hand shook and my stomach felt cold, as though an entire glass of ice water had sloshed into it.

The show must go on. Even if I wasn't part of it.

Father, I prayed as I walked out onto the stage, *help me get through this. Help me be strong enough to make one last sacrifice—to do the right thing once and for all in front of practically everyone I know.*

The spotlight hit me dead center and the music came up, swelling and fading as I walked to the floating glass podium. "Ladies and gentlemen, Regents, honored guests, and fellow students—hi and welcome to the Senior Cotillion of the graduating class of 2010!" Shrieks, cheers, and clapping as I punched the air. "My name is Lissa Mansfield, and as senior consultant for this event, the first thing I'd like to do is thank the hardworking team of juniors who put this together for you." More shrieks and cheers as behind me on the huge flat screen, the names of the people on my teams came up.

"I know we all want to get to the important part—the party!" Screams and cheering. "But it's our tradition to give a few awards before we get there. So without any more stalling, I'd like to announce the winner of the Debate Club's Student of the Year: Darcy Daniels!"

Darcy Daniels, a girl from my bio class with glasses and mouse-brown hair who could really have used a color rinse, lifted her tulle skirts and climbed the steps, where I presented her with her statuette. She was crying so hard her glasses fogged up, so I guided her to the side, where one of the band's roadies took her arm and made sure she didn't fall on her way back down.

Two more awards. Three. And then it was time.

With a gulp, I picked up the Board of Regents Honors statuette engraved with my name. "And now, I'm delighted to present Spencer Academy's highest honor for Service to the School to a girl who truly deserves it. Vanessa Talbot, come on up here!"

Silence, heavy with uncertainty.

Down at my table, bless their sweet hearts, everyone began to clap. The tables where the teachers and staff sat picked it up, and, holding the little gold statue, I began to clap, too.

From the back of the room, Vanessa made her way to the stage, and by the time she was halfway there, discretion had become the better part of valor and nearly everyone was clapping. After all, if the most popular girls in school were going to recognize her, it was smart not to buck the tide, right?

I met Vanessa in the spotlight and gave her my best Hollywood smile as I handed her the statuette. She turned it over, blinked, and shot me a puzzled glance.

"I'll explain later," I said, smiling even wider, and hugged her for good measure. "Thank you, everyone!" I said. "Now I'd like to welcome the band to the stage, and we'll have more awards to give at the break. Ladies and gentlemen, San Francisco's own Neckties!"

The band ran onstage to ecstatic shrieks and applause, and crashed into their first number as I tottered, half blinded from the spotlights, back to my table. I lost Vanessa and my statuette in the crowd as people surged onto the dance floor. Instead, Shani caught my elbow as I sank into a chair I hoped was mine.

"Lissa."

"I know," I said. "I think Ashley stole Vanessa's award to keep her off the stage. What else was I going to do?"

"You could have skipped her," Shani hissed, leaning close to me. "We could have sent someone to find it and given it to her in my batch at the break."

I shook my head. "Maybe. But it's done now."

She dropped her voice even further. "But, Lissa. You deserve your moment, too. You deserve for people to know you won Regents' Honors. What did you do—give her the one with your name on it?"

"I hope she plans to get it back to me."

"If she doesn't, I'm going to hunt her down and rip it out of her hands."

"Just leave it, Shani. I know I won. That's good enough for me."

"It's not good enough for me." Her eyes narrowed to slits and her tone sounded dangerous as she scanned the crowd. "That's twice you've been done out of an award you deserved."

"Aren't you going to dance?" Time to change the subject. "Everyone else is."

Gillian and Kaz are.

You-know-where would freeze over and the inhabitants would play hockey before I'd say *that* out loud. Before I'd let anyone know that, under the rose-petal bodice of my dress, my heart felt bruised. And under my sparkly blue eye makeup, it was all I could do not to cry.

This was supposed to be the biggest, happiest night of my life.

And all I wanted to do was fold up and bawl until it was time to leave for college. Maybe even longer.

TRUE TO HER WORD, Shani hunted Vanessa down and retrieved the little statue. But she didn't give it to me. Oh, no. The little plotter waited until the band took its break.

"Are we having a good time?" she yelled into the microphone like a combination of Fergie and Tyra. When the crowd screamed, she applauded them and said, "I'm Shani Hanna, and it's my pleasure to announce the rest of the award winners for tonight. Let's have a big round of applause for our first winner, tonight's hostess Lissa Mansfield, who's taking home the Board of Regents' Honors award and its ten thousand dollar scholarship!"

So there I was onstage again, hefting the little gold statuette in my hand for the second time and waving at the cheering crowd. I gave Shani a hug and ran offstage into the embrace of my parents.

"I'm so proud of you!" Mom said as she hugged me.

"Ten grand?" Dad asked. "That'll buy you your back-to-school clothes, I guess."

"Very funny, Gabe," Mom chided him. "It'll go for tuition and textbooks, and that's that."

"Come on, Winner's Mom." He grabbed her hand. "Let's dance. I can actually understand the words to this one."

Laughing, she followed him out onto the dance floor. I put the statuette next to my plate as if its placement mattered enormously, and arranged my evening bag next to it.

Sigh. Everyone was having such a good time out there.

"Want to dance, Lissa?" Derrik Vaughan held out his hand.

"Sure." It beat sitting like a wallflower in my pretty dress, and if Ashley had let him off the leash for one dance, who was I to turn him down?

He seemed happy enough, though, and talked about Ashley as though he really liked her. When he took me back to my table, Jeremy was there, and after him, Brett and I did a fast technopop number that lifted my spirits in spite of the fact that I could see Kaz and Gillian twisting and bumping a few feet away.

And then the band segued into a slow, romantic ballad. I smiled at Brett and said, "Guess you'd better find your lady for this one, huh? I want to live to see the sun come up."

He laughed and we joined Carly, who whirled out onto the floor in his arms. So romantic, those two. Just like Shani and Danyel, locked together on the edge of the crowd, Shani's eyes blissfully closed as she danced with her cheek on Danyel's shoulder.

Well, at least I'd had a few dances. Never let it be said that the most popular girl in school was a complete wallfl—

"Would you like to dance, Lissa?" His voice made my stomach jump.

"It's a slow one." *Stupid! What made you say that?*

"I'm willing to take the risk if you are."

Okay, that sounded normal. I rose and let Kaz lead me out onto the floor, where I stepped into a waltz hold the way I'd done in five hundred dance classes with him as my partner.

"Whoa. You want the band to start throwing drumsticks at us? Relax." He changed the hold, sliding his arm around my waist and holding my right hand in his left, close to his heart.

Ohmigosh, he smelled good. As soon as I got back to the privacy of my own room in Santa Barbara, I was seriously buying a whole bottle of whatever he was wearing and dousing a pillow with it.

"Are you and Gillian having a good time?" I'd say anything at this point. Anything to distract myself from the fact that I could feel the warmth of his body right through his tux and my dress. Or maybe that was me, heating up ten degrees at a time just from being this close to the boy I wanted.

"As good a time as a person can have when each one wants to be with someone else."

"Huh?" Had someone spiked my ice water? Because that was the last thing I'd expected to hear.

"Gillian's a lot of fun and I really like her," he went on, his voice low and soft by my ear. "But I said 'Look at the pretties' when we came in, and she just looked at me funny."

"She wouldn't know that line was from the 'Shindig' episode because she doesn't watch *Firefly*," I reminded him. "If you'd said something about the fiber content in her dress being consistent with something found at a crime scene, then you'd have gotten her attention."

"You'd have understood."

"There's a lot I haven't understood lately," I said. "I've been completely stupid about some things."

"You? The Regents' Whatever winner? I'd say you'd have to have some smarts going on."

"Not when it comes to you." Bone-scraping honesty time. "I screwed up, Kaz, and I'm really sorry."

"Yeah?"

"You told me what you wanted and I ran away like a little girl. I know it's too late, but I wanted you to know that I've grown up over the last couple of weeks."

"Yeah?"

I waited for a moment, in case he wanted to add something to that. "Is that all you can say? Yeah?"

"I'm trying to have me a dance, here, Lissa. A nice slow dance."

"That you should be having with your girlfriend."

"Mm. I'm working on that."

Which meant I spent the rest of the night trying to figure out all the ways he could possibly mean what I hoped he meant.

chapter 23

THE BOYS KIDNAPPED US at a quarter past midnight.

With Brett and Carly, Shani and Danyel in Brett's rumbling vintage Camaro, and Kaz, Jeremy, Gillian, and me in Danyel's truck, we took the highway over the hills past the San Andreas Fault zone, heading for the beach.

My parents knew I was with Kaz and that we were going somewhere for an afterparty. I don't know what Gillian's parents thought of the plan. They probably thought Gillian was safely tucked up in her bed when instead, she was crushed up against the passenger door, laughing at Jeremy, who was smooshed into the jumpseat behind us.

Gillian against the door, you say? In that case, who was sitting next to Kaz?

That would be me, shoes kicked off, trying to keep my sky-blue skirts from wrapping around the gear shift. While Kaz and Jeremy sang along to the raucous Switchfoot song in the CD changer, I leaned a subtle elbow into Gillian's side.

"Mind telling me what's going on here?"

"You haven't figured it out?"

"I don't know what to think anymore. Are you going out with him or not?"

"Not, of course, you goof. It was all a clever ploy to make you jealous."

"Very clever. It totally worked. You're lucky to be alive and not in little pieces in the rain tunnel."

She laughed and joined in the singing while the taillights of the Camaro crested the last hill and headed toward the silver sheet of the ocean below. As the truck went up and over the crest behind it, I felt like flying up into the sky and bursting into fireworks. Maybe I'd be mad at them later for messing with my mind, but right now I was too happy. It was nearly one o'clock in the morning of the first day of life after high school, which meant it was a time for forgiveness and new beginnings.

And a beach fire and moonlight.

And nearly all of my favorite people in the world.

We parked in an empty lot perched on an overlook. Danyel and Kaz had come prepared with blankets and sticks of wood to build a fire, and Brett pulled a picnic basket out of the trunk. Wow.

"I think this was planned," I murmured to Carly.

"I think it's sweet of them. Not to mention Mrs. L. She put together the food."

We settled onto the blankets as the boys got the fire going. I know, I know. I'm perfectly capable of building a beach fire. But somehow it was all part of the beauty of the night—the wash of the waves, the moon riding high in the sky, and the guys we cared about being all manly and taking care of us as we spread the skirts of our pretty dresses on the blankets.

Danyel had brought his guitar, of course. I'll never hear

"Seven Spanish Angels" again without hearing Shani's sweet harmony blending with his voice, the waves beating slow time in the background, and seeing the firelight sparkling in Gillian's and Carly's eyes.

Jeremy sat next to Gillian, but there was no awkwardness between them. I mean, she'd gone to Cotillion as Kaz's date, and you'd sort of think that would bother him, wouldn't you? But Jeremy is made of strong stuff. Gillian had drawn the line, not without pain for both of them, and her friendship was so important to him that he was willing to live on the other side of it, extending a hand for support.

So the fact that they were easy with each other made me feel easy, too. Not that I was completely relaxed. How could I be, with Kaz lounging next to me close enough to touch? I leaned back on my hands, singing when I remembered the words, and humming when I didn't, aware every second of his hand two inches from mine.

Was he leaving the next step up to me? Or should I go along with the gallant theme of the evening and let him make the first move?

I felt like one of those cliff divers in Acapulco. Imagine taking your first real dive, standing there on the rocks and looking down what seems to be miles to the surface of the ocean. Sure, you'd know that generations of divers had done it before you, but this is *you*, with practice behind you but no real experience. You'd be the one to either plunge in, or be the one to find a submerged rock that would end your hopes for good.

So you make a choice. You can retrace your steps back up the path and give up cliff diving forever. Or you can close your eyes, take a big breath, and launch yourself in a perfect swan dive, out into the black.

I moved my fingers and touched Kaz's hand.

The cliff diver finds himself falling, falling, and then being embraced by the deep water. *It's you. It's me. It's us.*

Kaz's hand opened with no hesitation at all, his fingers sliding along mine in a clasp that was warm and sure and erased the last of the insecurity and doubt lurking in the dark corners of my heart.

On the other side of the fire, Carly looked from our linked hands to my face. Her eyes sparkled as she caught Shani's and Gillian's attention. Danyel and Brett were singing now, which meant they were conveniently distracted as Carly transmitted the good news with a lift of her eyebrow and a smile.

On my other side, Gillian bumped my shoulder with hers in a gesture that plainly said, *My work here is done. I'm so happy.*

Kaz fought a smile. He's no dummy. He can read a glance as well as I can, especially when it's about him. "Are you cold?" he asked me. "We have another blanket in the truck."

I opened my mouth to say no, when Gillian bumped my shoulder again.

Oh. Oh, my. Get with the program, Lissa.

"A blanket would be good," I said. "I'll come with you."

Feeling as obvious as a thief caught on a security tape, I picked up my skirts in one hand and walked with Kaz back across the beach toward the short slope of the cliff. Without a word, he took my other hand . . . and in that warm clasp, I understood a bunch of things.

I'm glad we're here.

No more misunderstanding.

It's you. It's me.

It's us.

He helped me up the rocky slope to the parking lot. The

truck sat under a windblown pine that cast a deep shadow on the driver's side. I leaned on the door.

"I don't really need a blanket."

"I know. But it was a good excuse to get you over here alone." My stomach jumped and goosebumps prickled along my arms. "Hey, you really are cold."

"I'm not." My voice dropped. "I'm—I'm kind of nervous."

He let out a long breath. "I'm glad it's not just me."

The rueful bend in his mouth and his funny little confession startled a laugh out of me. "We're not supposed to be scared of each other."

"It's not like that. But . . ." He moved closer. So close I could feel the heat from his body once more, warming me better than any blanket. "I've been imagining this for so long, and now it's here—I mean, you're here and I'm here and . . ."

I put a finger on his lips. "Hey. It's us."

He leaned his forehead on mine and looked into my eyes. "I'm glad it's us."

"It always has been, you know. No matter who I was going out with, or who you were going out with, it's been you the whole time."

"Even when you didn't know it?"

"Especially then."

"You're not making sense."

"I don't feel very sensible. I feel . . ."

"What?"

"Happy. Like God has been waiting all this time for me to open a present. And the present was you."

"Is the future me, too?"

Trust Kaz to turn a word on its head, even at a moment like this. "I hope so. I think so."

"Lissa?"

"Yes?"

"Are you going to stop talking and let me kiss you?"

My heart felt like it would burst with joy.

It's him. It's me. It's the God we love together. It's the power of friendship and the gifts it brings us every day.

"Are you going to kiss me and make me stop talking?"

I could feel the smile on his lips as he bent down and, for the first time, did exactly that.

about the author

Shelley Adina wrote her first teen novel when she was thirteen. It was rejected by the literary publisher to whom she sent it, but he did say she knew how to tell a story. That was enough to keep her going through the rest of her adolescence, a career, a move to another country, a B.A. in Literature, an M.A. in Writing Popular Fiction, and countless manuscript pages.

Shelley is a world traveler and pop culture junkie with an incurable addiction to designer handbags. She knows the value of a relationship with a gracious God and loving Christian friends and loves writing about fun and faith—with a side of glamour. Between books, Shelley loves traveling, listening to and making music, and watching all kinds of movies.

The Fruit of My Lipstick

New Yorker Gillian Chang starts her second term at posh Spencer Academy boarding school in San Francisco prepared to focus on her studies, her faith, and her friends—Lissa Mansfield and Carly Aragon. She plays half a dozen musical instruments and can recite the periodic table of the elements backward. She's totally prepared for everything—except love!

She's falling hard for Lucas Hayes, a junior who is already aiming at a PhD in physics from Stanford. The problem is, she never seems to be able to measure up and be the girlfriend he wants. He's under a lot of pressure to achieve— maybe that's why he's short-tempered sometimes. But even a thick-skinned girl like Gillian can only take so much.

With her heart on the line, Gillian conceals more and more from her friends. So when she's accused of selling exam answer sheets, even Lissa and Carly wonder if it's true. Can Gillian hang on to her integrity—and her faith—when she loses her heart to Lucas?

Be Strong & Curvaceous

After spending spring break in Mexico with her grandparents, Carly Aragon can't wait to get back to school at Spencer Academy in San Francisco. With Lissa Mansfield and Gillian Chang by her side, she's ready for anything . . . except a new roommate.

Lady Lindsay MacPhail, flamboyant daughter of the Earl of Strathcairn, quickly becomes Carly's worst nightmare. "Mac" not only swoops in and steals Carly's privacy, she also sets her sights on Brett Loyola—Carly's biggest crush!

But when Mac starts receiving strange, threatening e-mails, she and Carly must come together to figure out who's behind them and why. In the end, the fate of one girl will lie in the other's hands. Will the two learn to trust one another and trust God?

DON'T FORGET TO GRAB BOOK FOUR
IN THE SERIES:

Who Made You a Princess?

Shani returns to Spencer Academy after an amazing summer with her friends and a new hottie: Danyel Johnstone. The two are just starting to generate some heat when it's time to hit the books again. But a new addition to the student body has all the girls buzzing. Prince Rashid al Amir is doing an exchange term at Spencer Academy—and he's set his sights on Shani.

It turns out that Shani's family and the prince's go back for generations. In each generation, members of the two families have expanded their business interests through an archaic and inescapable tradition. Will Shani put aside her feelings for Danyel to become a princess? Or will her headstrong ways put her feelings, her future, and her faith at risk?

AVAILABLE AT BOOKSTORES NOW!

Tidings of Great Boys

Finals week is approaching and Mac is still undecided on where to spend the holidays. Normally she'd go home to Scotland, but spending two weeks alone in the castle with her dad isn't as appealing as it used to be. So she invites Carly, Lissa, Gillian, and Shani to join her for the holidays!

Mac is determined to make this the best Christmas ever. She even decides to organize the traditional Hogmanay dance for New Year's Eve. If she can get her mother involved, maybe her parents will finally get back together.

But when Mac and the girls arrive in Scotland, they are faced with bad news: the castle is falling apart and Mac's parents are struggling financially. Not only that, but Shani is in big trouble with Prince Rashid's royal family. Can the girls find a way to celebrate the holidays, get Mac's parents back together, save the castle, and rescue Shani . . . and will Mac believe it's all part of God's plan? There's only one way to find out!